AN UNSUITABLE SUITOR

A REGENCY ROMANCE NOVELLA

SALLY BRITTON

An
Unsuitable
Suitor

SALLY BRITTON

Published by Pink Citrus Books | Edited by Molly Holt, Edits by Molly
Proofread by Carri Flores | Cover design by Blue Water Books

An earlier version of this story was published in *An Evening at Almack's,* Timeless Regency Collection Book 12 on March 19, 2019, titled *The Heart's Choice.* This is a newly edited and expanded edition.

Sally Britton
www.authorsallybritton.com

First Printing: August 2021
Paperback ISBN: 978-1-68527-004-9
eBook ISBN: 978-1-68527-003-2

To My Sisters:
I'm glad we've always looked out for each other.

CHAPTER 1

LONDON, MARCH 1814

"*D*o stop dawdling, Matilda."

One would think, given Beatrice's tone, that Mattie was a delinquent child rather than the elder—and quite firmly the more responsible—of the two sisters.

"Stopping to greet our neighbors, especially those of respectable age and rank, is not dawdling," Mattie corrected, attempting to keep up with her younger sister.

"It is when we have better things to do." Beatrice sniffed but finally slowed her rather unladylike stride to look over her shoulder. "And when the person you stop to speak to is that horrid Lady Fenlock. You *know* she delights in spreading rumors about me."

Rumors that were, Mattie knew, very well founded. Beatrice had something of a reputation for being a flirt.

"She is also someone we need if we hope to be invited anywhere this Season." Mattie looked at her younger sister from the corner of her eye, studying the artful way Beatrice's sun-gold hair escaped her bonnet in playful ringlets. Her sister truly was lovely as Aphrodite and a contrast to Mattie in almost every way.

Mattie was older by four years, and at age twenty-six she didn't mind being considered on the shelf. Her hair was darker, her eyes muddier, and her complexion not so faultlessly pale as her sister's. Beatrice was tall and willowy, Mattie of an average height and shape. Beatrice could command a room with ease, and Mattie much preferred being an observer on the edges of most parties.

"As long as we have vouchers, we will do well enough," Beatrice argued. "We do not need old gossipy geese to beg us invitations, Matilda. We are attractive young ladies, daughters of nobility." She narrowed her eyes. "Our family has commanded respect for generations." Beatrice tilted her nose into the air and walked at a faster clip again.

It took a firm hold on her tongue to keep Mattie from replying to that remark. Managing Beatrice was far harder than managing the family's estate. The Granthorne barony had meant something for nearly a hundred years, but Mattie knew that in a single generation it could crumble like the ruins of their ancestors' castle. Should people discover their father's ailment, Beatrice's lack of propriety would not even be completely to blame.

Mattie's steps on the walk slowed as she considered her father's condition, one for which his doctor could give them no cure. Her heart ached at the thought of losing the man who had been her hero all her life. Her sister didn't seem to notice when Mattie fell behind.

If Mattie could persuade Beatrice to focus on one man long enough to marry her off, she just might salvage the family name, her father's dignity, and her mother's pride. Beatrice must stop being so stubborn about everything to do with marriage. Many of her worthier callers had disappeared after the previous year. Her sister, at twenty-two, didn't command the devotees she had at eighteen and nineteen. But there was one man who might do.

Mr. Arthur Redhurst, a gentleman of means if not in possession of a title, would make a fine husband for Miss Beatrice Rayment, younger daughter of the sixth Baron Granthorne. They would do well together. Both mothers—and Mattie—thought so.

While Mattie had been thinking, Beatrice walked ahead of her by nearly twenty yards, but Mattie refused to run to catch up. They were on the street of their townhouse, after all, and she could at least see her sister well enough to stop any real trouble from happening. Or so she thought, until she saw a gentleman had stopped on the walk, doffing his hat to speak with Beatrice.

Narrowing her eyes, Mattie maintained her even speed and tried to determine who the man was. He was tall and dark haired, and his words carried to her clearly in the air, in a voice as unexpected as it was familiar.

"Miss Beatrice, good afternoon. It is a pleasure to see you after so long."

It cannot be.

Standing before her eyes was none other than Oliver Bolton.

Beatrice curtsied, and Mattie slowed her step, only a few feet away now, waiting for her sister to identify the gentleman.

"Good afternoon," Beatrice said as she returned to her full height. "Pardon me, but how do you know my name? I do not believe we have met."

Beatrice raised a hand to her cheek, batting her eyelashes in her most coquettish manner. Mattie ground her teeth together. No. Beatrice must *not* be allowed to toy with this man's feelings, innocent flirtation or not.

"Oh, we've met, Miss Beatrice. In fact, I've known you for years. You do not know me?" He spoke with a lilt to his voice Mattie had always found rather charming. What on earth was he doing here, on their street? And how could Beatrice not recognize the man who had grown up practically on their doorstep?

Beatrice shook her head, tilting her head coyly. "Sir, I would remember meeting someone such as you. I never forget a handsome gentleman, and it is really too bad of you to pretend to know me. We must be properly introduced, or there will be gossip."

As one of their near neighbors was peering out her front window in that instant, Mattie knew there was a great deal of truth in that statement.

Mattie stepped forward, between her sister and the gentleman. "Oliver, how lovely to see you again." She curtsied, keeping her eyes on the nephew of their steward. "Forgive me. It is Mr. Bolton now we have all grow."

Oliver had come to live with his uncle after the deaths of his parents many years ago, thus forming an acquaintance with the Rayment sisters out of a polite sort of necessity. He'd been a sad, kind lad then, but he had matured into a handsome man. With him standing before her for the first time in years, grown into his new role of gentleman, Mattie decided he'd aged *excessively* well.

Beatrice's eyes grew wide and her lips parted in surprise. She seemed to be thinking much the same as Mattie had.

"Oliver Bolton? The steward's nephew?" The younger woman gasped. "I hardly recognize you."

Although he'd matured, all his former features remained much the same. If her sister didn't recognize the man, it was likely because she'd never paid him much attention in the first place. Oliver's slight frown seemed to indicate he might think the same.

Although Mattie had years of practice when it came to smoothing over her sister's manner, she now struggled to find the words to spare Oliver's feelings. "It is very good to see you, Mr. Bolton. I had no idea you were in London. It's going on five years since you went away from us." Mattie kept her smile merely polite, though her words were said with kindness. "How are you settling into your new life? I understand your estate in Lincolnshire takes up a great deal of your time."

The man's dark-green eyes glanced from her to Beatrice, but they settled more firmly on Mattie again when Beatrice continued to gape at him. "Westerwind did not take to me as quickly as I wished, but presently the lands and farms are doing well. It sounds as though my uncle has been keeping you at least somewhat informed as to my whereabouts."

Mattie was the only member of the family who had spoken to the steward in quite some time, and he was forever telling her of his nephew's successes.

"He is very proud of you, Mr. Bolton," she answered. "Of course he mentions you from time to time. It is good that you have such a source as Mr. Hapsbury to guide you. Our family would be quite lost without him." The truth of that statement weighed upon her heart.

Mattie chanced a glance in her sister's direction to see if Beatrice had composed herself yet. The speculative gleam in Beatrice's eyes made Mattie's stomach clench. Mattie knew that look. She'd seen it all her life, from the time Beatrice was a child and discovered a toy she coveted.

"Beatrice, darling," she said, hoping her tone was warning enough for her sister that *this* was not a man whose affections were a plaything. "We ought to return home and see if Lady Sefton has replied to our request for vouchers." Mattie had received hints from the patroness that they would be permitted to enter the upper ballroom, where they had been denied the previous year for reasons unknown to any but the patronesses themselves.

"Yes, of course." Beatrice adjusted the reticule on her wrist but looked up at Oliver through her eyelashes in a manner that rather reminded Mattie of a puppy begging for scraps. Unfortunately, the men of London seemed inclined to like puppies. "Will *you* be applying for vouchers to Almack's, Mr. Bolton?" Beatrice asked.

Oliver's smile diminished.

Mattie nearly panicked but remained composed. Someone of Oliver's standing wouldn't be likely to gain admission to Almack's. He wouldn't have enough connections or funds, and Beatrice ought to know that. Asking him so directly was akin to offering an insult.

"I am afraid not, Miss Beatrice. But I do hope you enjoy yourself at the balls. If you will excuse me, Miss Rayment, Miss Beatrice." He bowed and replaced his hat with an air of gravity. "I hope to see you again soon."

"Good day, Mr. Bolton," Mattie said, giving Beatrice no time to ask more questions. She took her sister's arm and tugged her down the walkway, fixing her eyes on their front door.

Hopefully that would be the last they would see of Oliver Bolton. But a strange premonition made her think that wish was in vain. Oliver had always been a well-mannered boy, and he would likely come to the house to call on their father. Even a gesture as well-meant as that could be disastrous for all of them.

"I wonder if Mr. Redhurst has sent you flowers today,"

Mattie said, as cheerily as possible, in an effort to divert her sister.

"He sends flowers nearly every day," Beatrice responded, boredom coloring her words.

This will never do. Mattie took in a deep breath and launched into speaking with excitement about Almack's, Mr. Redhurst, and the last few months of the Season. Beatrice knew full well that she needed to wed a gentleman of some standing this Season or risk remaining a spinster. But she had certainly done precious little to help the situation, other than flirt with half the men in Society.

If Beatrice became distracted by Oliver Bolton before being properly engaged, it may well ruin her standing in Mr. Redhurst's eyes. Before their return to the country, Mattie *had* to see her sister safely married. The family depended upon it.

CHAPTER 2

"Tell me again: why must I attend this party with you?" Oliver asked his friend for the second time in as many days. "I am not certain this is the correct place for me to begin my foray into London society."

"It is the perfect way to begin, Bolton. An intimate card party, with the most well-connected guests in attendance, will give you the right sort of introductions." Robert Dunwilde, heir to an earldom, grinned across the coach from Oliver. "And it's a little late to bow out now, isn't it?" he asked as their carriage arrived at the house of the party in question.

Oliver folded his arms across his chest, tucking his hands beneath them. If he didn't force his hands still, he knew he'd fiddle with his cravat, a nervous habit which caused his recently acquired valet despair on nearly a daily basis.

"They will think me an upstart."

Dunwilde waved away Oliver's concerns. "It is the perfect place to find elegant young ladies to keep you company. You worry too much. Enjoy yourself a little."

It was easy for Dunwilde to say. The man was heir to a

fortune, a title, and had a standing in society Oliver could never hope to obtain. Oliver Bolton, on the other hand, was the son of a deceased merchant and the nephew of a steward, had never gone away to school, and bore the new gilt of a country gentleman.

Oliver followed his friend through an entry hall, relinquishing his hat and greatcoat to a waiting footman. He tried to meet the servant's eye, wondering if this man in his fine livery could guess how similar their lives had been but five years before.

The servant accepted Oliver's things, bowed, and departed without a word.

Dunwilde had vanished, and the other guests were making their way up the main staircase to the first floor, where they would play cards and drink as though nothing in the world could ever trouble them. He sucked in a deep breath, trying to draw courage from the empty air around him.

The large upstairs parlor he entered was full of tables, laughter, and no sign of Dunwilde. Oliver's gaze swept from one side of the room to the other, desperately seeking someone he might know, but—

The warm glow of honey-colored hair attracted his eye, and he took in the young woman with surprise.

It couldn't be. Twice in the same day.

Perhaps the fabled Fates of the ancient world were smiling upon him after all. Miss Beatrice stood near a window, looking out over the party with her bewitching blue eyes. Years before, when she was seventeen, she had danced across his romantic daydreams. She'd been a delightful child, four years his junior, an enchanting youth with an easy laugh, and then she'd burst into womanhood and stolen his fancy.

Five years ago, she'd been beyond his reach. But now, seeing her twice in one day, he wondered if such might no longer be true.

She met his eyes from across the room, and it was as though she issued a challenge when their gazes collided.

Without further thought, he went to her. He wound his way through the tables, taking notice of nothing else. Her lashes dropped as he drew nearer.

"Good evening, Miss Beatrice." He held his breath, waiting, watching her closely for any sign of his welcome. She returned his bow with the slightest dip of a curtsy.

"Mr. Bolton, what a pleasant surprise. I hope you are not offended by my lack of recognition this afternoon." She studied his face with earnestness, her eyebrows furrowing in a most adorable manner.

Initially, that had disappointed Oliver. But he chose to view it as a compliment. He stood taller and tugged at his sleeves.

"Oh, I suppose I have grown rather dashing."

She fluttered her eyelashes at him, and a coy smile appeared. "I absolutely agree with you. You are quite changed for the better."

"Mr. Bolton," a voice said at his elbow, startling him. He turned, looking down into the solemn eyes of another woman from his past. It would be easy to resent Matilda's sudden appearance, given that he longed for an opportunity to speak with Beatrice alone. Yet Matilda's unceasing kindness towards him made it impossible to hold anything against the woman.

"It is wonderful to see you again, Miss Rayment." Oliver bowed.

"Indeed. The pleasure is mine. How delightful to see you twice in one day," she said, her words and look at odds with each other. She certainly didn't *appear* pleased to see him, but as to why, Oliver was uncertain.

Matilda turned away before he could respond, addressing her sister. "I understand Mr. Redhurst will not be attending tonight. He sent a note that his sister is unwell."

Although immediately curious as to who this Mr. Redhurst was and why his attendance mattered, Oliver couldn't help being gratified when Beatrice showed no disappointment at the news.

"I suppose he is a very attentive brother." Beatrice hardly reacted and, without another word on the matter, turned her attention right back to Oliver. "Mr. Bolton, won't you join me in a game of whist?"

Flattered to be the object of her focus, he extended his arm to her. "It would be my great pleasure, Miss Beatrice." He didn't give a thought to Matilda until they'd taken two steps away, then turned to see her staring after them. "Would you like to join us, Miss Rayment?"

Beatrice laughed. "Matilda isn't a great hand at cards. She's far too serious to enjoy the game." When Matilda's only reaction to her sister's words was to arch her eyebrows, he took that as indication enough she would not mind them stepping away.

Oliver quietly admired Beatrice and the way her curls framed her pretty face, counting himself fortunate to spend an evening in her company. Years ago, she'd hardly known he existed.

Perhaps stepping from one rung on the social ladder up to another wouldn't be as difficult as he'd thought.

Mattie watched her sister all evening with concern. In Beatrice's first Season, she had gathered male admirers as a child gathers daisies in a field, whimsically and without much thought. Her father declared her too young to marry, and Beatrice hadn't minded the idea of another Season of such entertainment and admiration.

During Beatrice's second Season, Mattie had been the only one in the family to disapprove of her sister's more calculated tactics in attracting the attentions of unattached young men. Father and Mother had both been certain their darling daughter would make a match most brilliant, for everyone thought Beatrice to be lovely and charming.

Mattie, therefore, was the only one unsurprised when Beatrice declared she had no wish to marry any of her swains and even *turned away* two serious proposals of marriage to perfectly decent young men. Her reason?

"I have no wish to settle into the dull existence of a wife when I could be dancing every night," she had explained.

Watching her sister flirt with Oliver Bolton, a handsome man if Mattie had ever seen one, left the elder sister slightly nauseated. And she could not shake the feeling, as he gave Beatrice his full attention and made her giggle at the card table, that a disaster brewed before her very eyes.

While Beatrice had been oblivious to Oliver in the past, Mattie had, in fact, always admired him. Mattie had often observed the unfortunate boy and thought his circumstances quite tragic. He was as clever as his uncle, their steward, and was taller and finer looking than the sons of the surrounding gentry. The thing she admired most about him was how he always had a kind word for everyone. Yet, he was an orphan, uneducated, and without many prospects for his future.

She recalled he had always looked out for her sister with

a great deal of earnestness. Protectiveness, perhaps, when they were younger. But what if it had been more? It certainly looked like a different sort of emotion at present.

Oliver gazed at her sister with an admiration she had seen on many a gentleman's face. Mr. Bolton, nephew of their steward, was enamored with Beatrice.

It would not do.

Beatrice had built a relationship with Mr. Redhurst, a man of wealth and consequence.

Mr. Redhurst, Mattie thought, might even be persuaded to marry her younger sister. He'd paid her every attention and seemed to understand her nature enough to make allowances for her spirited nature.

Beatrice absolutely *had* to marry, and soon. With their father's failing health, and the entailment of his properties to a distant cousin, the Mrs. and Misses Rayments could soon be without a home. But if Mattie could help her sister secure a safe home, then at least all would be well for Beatrice. Perhaps for their mother, too.

Mattie turned over her sister's character in her mind. As long as Mr. Redhurst didn't see evidence of Beatrice's somewhat fickle nature, and if he attended the next event with them, likely Beatrice's attention would focus back where it ought to be.

Oliver Bolton's deep-green eyes, dark, curling hair, and strong jaw might amuse Beatrice for a short while, but Mattie hoped that was all he would be. A brief distraction.

Lady Granthorne came across the room, smiling at her acquaintances as she went, then stood near the wall with Mattie. She opened her fan and spoke, low enough only her daughter could hear.

"Who is that young man with Beatrice?" How could her mother not recognize him? Mattie had known him at once.

"Oliver Bolton. Mr. Hapsbury's nephew."

Her mother's mouth turned downward in a severe frown, hidden from all but Mattie by her fan. "The steward's nephew? The one who went away to inherit something?"

"An estate, Mother."

"Dear me. And what is he to Beatrice?"

"An inconsequential conquest, I'm certain." Mattie forced a smile, even as she heard her sister's laughter ring as clearly as a bell. "Beatrice has Mr. Redhurst's interests. She will not forget him easily."

"Let us hope," her mother said, narrowing her eyes.

Mattie nodded, distracted by Oliver's pleasant laugh and the fond way he gazed at her sister.

As much as Mattie had always liked Oliver, she could not allow him to distract Beatrice. The flighty young woman needed stability, and their family needed to maintain a level of respectability that a man in possession of a small estate in Lincolnshire could not hope to attain. Beatrice, used to living in a grand style, would not do well with a man whose fortune required a more moderate outlook, and likely kept him in the country far more than allowed him sojourn in London.

"Of course," her mother continued in an airy manner, "you could always marry, Matilda."

Mattie didn't deign to reply to that absurd suggestion. She was much too old to marry now. She had been unsuccessful in finding love or a situation which would offer comfort enough to induce her to wed without true affection.

"I know what you are thinking, dear." Her mother flicked her fan closed, her expression turning gentle. "It isn't too late for you to find someone. I promise it isn't."

"It's of no consequence, Mother." Mattie pretended her glove need adjusting. "When the time comes, I will find a position that suits me." They had already discussed who Mattie might apply to as a lady's companion, though teaching at a seminary for girls wasn't out of the question.

"I cannot think you will be happy that way," Mother murmured, her eyes growing dark in her worry.

Happiness for her sister and mother's security would have to be enough. "I am far too practical to worry over such things, especially at the moment. Beatrice is the only one either of us need to worry over."

"As you say, Matilda." Her mother stood next to her in quiet, the buzz of conversations in the room the only sound passing between them.

Matilda didn't release the sigh that built up in her lungs. Not all at once, in a huff. But slowly. Then she managed a smile for her mother's sake. "I am well, Mother. You should enjoy the evening. Isn't that one of your friends, just come into the room?"

"Oh, yes. Lady Topley is here. Excuse me, my dear." Her mother gave Matilda's hand a gentle squeeze before she glided away, a picture of grace despite her forty-six years. No one in their social circle would ever suppose the baroness to be suffering through the difficulties that plagued their family.

CHAPTER 3

*O*liver came to pay a morning call to Miss Beatrice, a true spring in his step. He'd hardly slept the night before, busy as his mind had been in conjuring up Beatrice's delightful laugh and the way she'd looked up at him through her eyelashes. The attention she'd lavished upon him the previous evening, speaking to practically no one else, had done much to encourage him.

The last time he'd had the privilege of Beatrice's company had been just before her seventeenth birthday. Her dancing instructor had despaired over the young woman's lack of ability with the minuet and enlisted Oliver and Matilda to practice the forms. Oliver, barely a passable dancer himself, added to the confusion in the family's music room by stepping on Beatrice's hem and nearly knocking Matilda over.

The dancing master had railed at him, calling him an oaf, but Beatrice had laughed the matter away, and Matilda whispered the correct steps to him the remainder of their practice.

Did Beatrice remember that day?

He presented his card to the butler and waited in the hall, wondering if he would be shown upstairs or if the family were not yet receiving callers.

The steady clop of shoes on marble made Oliver straighten, but it was Lord Granthorne who appeared from the corridor, looking about as though searching for someone.

Oliver's interactions with the baron had been infrequent. He'd spoken to Lord Granthorne in his uncle's office when they'd discussed estate matters, and never in a more informal setting. If his uncle had spoken to Matilda of his letters, he must've mentioned Oliver's progress and prospects to the baron as well.

"Where are they?" the baron muttered, barely loud enough for Oliver to hear. "They must be around here somewhere."

Oliver cleared his throat, realizing the baron remained unaware of his presence. "Good afternoon, my lord."

The baron's steps halted, and his forehead scrunched, dim blue eyes narrowing. "Who's that?" he asked, voice accusing rather than curious or welcoming. "What do you want?"

Oliver, taken aback, bowed deeply. "I beg your pardon, my lord. I am Oliver Bolton. I've come to call on your daughter."

The older man came forward, his steps swift, and held his hands out in greeting. "Yes, yes. Welcome. Mattie is an exceptional young lady. She will be pleased you've come to see her. Wasn't she stunning last evening? The ball. It was a spectacle, was it not?"

"The ball?" Oliver's forehead wrinkled, and he studied Lord Granthorne, confused.

"Yes. Mattie has a fine pair of feet for dancing. You must agree with me. I will also say she has me to thank for that.

We've been dancing together since she was a tiny thing." The baron chuckled, then raised a hand to his forehead and rubbed at it, his eyes dimming. "She isn't small any longer, is she?"

Uncertain as to what response he ought to make, and hesitant to correct his lordship that it had been a card party and not a ball, Oliver began to nod his agreement when a voice from above called down.

"Papa, there you are." Matilda, holding the rail at the top of the steps, seemed to take in the scene in the entryway before she came swiftly down to the ground floor, speaking all the while. "Mother was looking for you. She needs your opinion on the menu for your birthday."

"My birthday. Yes." Lord Granthorne's expression altered from thoughtful to surprised. "I had best tell her not to serve fish." Without another word to either of them, he hurried up the steps, calling out as he went, "I cannot abide fish most days, but certainly not on my birthday."

Matilda watched him go, her dark brows drawn together and a wistful sort of gleam in her eyes. Her bronze hair, pulled up and away from her face in an intricately twisted chignon, had a tiny white feather caught in it. This presumably misplaced feather momentarily distracted him from the situation at hand.

"When is your father's birthday?" he asked, then bit his tongue. He hadn't even properly greeted her yet. "I beg your pardon, Miss Rayment." He bowed, taking his eye away from the wispy feather. "I have come to pay a call to your sister, er—and to you."

"Of course, Mr. Bolton. I received your card and came to speak to you myself. Please, come into the room here." She gestured to a door off the entry, and he preceded her through it into a small sitting room with dark furnishings and a large desk. A study? Not the usual place to show a guest, at all.

A couch near the hearth was the only comfortable seating, and that is where she led him. "Won't you sit down?"

With his hat and gloves still in hand, as the butler hadn't returned to retrieve them, Oliver lowered himself onto the stiff cushions. Nothing about the situation made any sense. Either he ought to have been shown to an upstairs parlor or he should've been turned away.

Oliver rested his hat atop his lap, leaving enough space for her to sit, but Matilda began to pace across the rug before him, her hands clasped before her. Her movement made the feather in her hair wave with each step.

"Mr. Bolton, we have known each other a very long time. I have a great respect for your uncle, and his position, and I am genuinely happy for your change in fortune." Though she said each word kindly, there was a sternness to them that made his insides tighten.

"It sounds as though you are about to follow those pleasant sentiments with something far less amicable, Miss Rayment." He leaned back against the couch and crossed his arms, still gripping his gloves in one hand.

Her hands unclasped to run down the front of her dress, then she tucked them behind herself as she faced him. "I am afraid I must offer some caution, Mr. Bolton. As we *have* known each other for many years, I am in possession of several memories of the way you admired my sister before you left us for Lincolnshire. I confess, I watched last night to see if any of that regard remained." Her words halted, and she looked down at the carpet.

At least this conversation discomfited her as much as it did him. "What did you see, Miss Rayment?"

Matilda released her hands again and made a helpless gesture toward him. "You still hold a great deal of fondness for her, Mr. Bolton. I believe the whole room must have noticed."

"Then they noticed her attentions toward me were just as *fond*, I should think." Oliver would not allow her to make him feel guilty about spending the entirety of the evening with Beatrice. "Was there something in our conduct you personally object to, Miss Rayment?"

The woman before him took a step closer to him, her coppery eyes giving away nothing of her thoughts, but her hands were worrying themselves before her again. "No. My parents, on the other hand, are quite concerned over it. You see, there is a gentleman who is near to making an offer for Beatrice's hand. There is the fear that you, an old acquaintance, will disrupt their relationship."

"It must not be that firm of a connection if the nephew of your steward could hold sway over such an understanding." Oliver did his best to appear unconcerned, to show no fear in the face of the coming rejection. "May I ask why you, and not your father, would address me with these troublesome concerns? This seems like a conversation for the head of the family to attend, rather than the eldest daughter."

Her cheeks colored, but other than that rosy hue she appeared no less confident. "I thought to approach you as a friend, Mr. Bolton, to speak to you on these matters before things grew complicated." She abruptly came to the couch and sat down next to him, turning her body to face his. Her tone softened. "I adore my sister, Mr. Bolton, but as you may remember, Beatrice has a way about her not everyone understands. She also has a particular taste for the finer things of life which can be difficult to sustain."

Oliver narrowed his eyes, his reply quick and defensive.

"Are you doubting my abilities to provide the life she deserves? I assure you, there will be no issue." This caused him to pause and wonder if the words coming out of his mouth were true. With all the hard work he had put into his inherited estate, surely Beatrice could see his potential. "Besides, Miss Beatrice is a delightful young woman and has always been kind to me."

"Of course," she agreed readily, disarming him. "Beatrice has a gentle heart, but she also possesses a stubborn soul. I am afraid she can be decidedly impractical."

"Not like you," he interrupted, unable to help himself. "You have always been an impeccable example of practicality." Even as a girl, Matilda pursued interests in the running of a household rather than taking the time to enjoy entertainment or the company of others her age. When he'd come to live with his uncle, he and Matilda had both been twelve years old. She'd sought him out nearly at once to offer her condolences on the loss of his parents, with all the gravity a girl of that age could possess.

He'd both hated and appreciated the gesture for years. He never could decide if she had done it out of self-importance and some sort of curiosity regarding grief, or if she'd genuinely meant to be sympathetic.

She had nearly the same air about her today as she had at their first meeting from all those years before.

"Are you here to warn me away from her?" he asked, reluctant to allow her to guide the conversation further. "Were you appointed, as a *friend*, to tell me my attentions are unwanted?"

Matilda tipped her head to one side, her eyes shining at him. "What if I did such a thing? If I told you to leave, to refrain from seeking out my sister again, what would you do?"

"I am not merely a steward's nephew any longer, Miss Rayment. I am a gentleman of some means, though they are modest compared to your father's. I am not going to disappear back to Lincolnshire because you wish it. I am in London to create new connections and plan my future. Your sister is old enough to make up her own mind about me, or the man your family intends for her. I am not going anywhere." He tensed, prepared to stand and leave the room when she dismissed him.

Her gentle smile stopped him.

"Bravo, Mr. Bolton. Those are honorable words, and I respect your position. I am glad to find you a man of principle. Very well. I wish you good fortune in your endeavors." She stood, her skirts brushing the edge of his shoes.

He remained sitting, too befuddled to do more than look up at her. "You do not object to me paying a call on your sister?"

"I would never discourage someone so earnest and sincere as you have shown yourself to be," she said firmly. "Though I am afraid it will have to wait. Beatrice is not home at present. She has gone shopping with a friend. We are to go to Almack's this evening, and Beatrice is in need of a new fan." Matilda gestured to the door, her true thoughts still concealed behind intelligent eyes and a tight-lipped smile. "You may wait in the upstairs parlor, if you wish, but I must warn you that she can be about such things for the entirety of an afternoon."

He'd nearly forgotten it was Wednesday. Every member of society would be preparing for an evening at Almack's or else would spend the day pretending they didn't care to attend, because they had been unable to obtain vouchers.

"Perhaps I could facilitate an outing with my sister, if you wish."

Startled by her suggestion, it took Oliver a moment to answer. What was the woman playing at? He'd been certain her purpose in their rather strange tête-à-tête was to warn him to leave her sister alone. Perhaps now he had her approval.

Though he would do well to exercise some caution until he understood the situation. "What did you have in mind?"

"Beatrice enjoys the theater. If you can secure tickets, perhaps this Friday?"

Oliver tucked his hat beneath his arm and ran his gloved hand through his hair. "You are encouraging my association with your sister, Miss Rayment?"

"As you said, you are both capable of knowing your own minds. Beatrice is nearly of age. Though I must warn you"—Matilda paused, twisting her fingers together—"Beatrice does enjoy collecting admirers." Matilda's expression seemed almost wistful, for the barest moment before she turned away to face the hearth.

Her statement didn't surprise him. Though he'd been away from the family's society for some years, Beatrice had always possessed a mischievous nature. Her flirting with him at the card party supported Matilda's words.

"Thank you, Miss Rayment. I will attend to your sister in two days' time, for the theater." He bowed but paused midway through the motion. "Do *you* like the theater, Miss Rayment?"

She cast him a confused look over her shoulder. "I? Do I like it? Yes, of course."

"Perhaps you could attend with us," he said, hoping a polite invitation could further win over the woman's approval. The more that Miss Rayment liked him, the more likely it was that Beatrice would as well.

"Thank you, but I—" She cut her words off, her eyebrows furrowing. "I would not wish to intrude. We can find another chaperone."

"You would be most welcome, not as a chaperone, but as a friend. After all, we have known each other a very long time." He grinned, using her words against her.

Though she didn't laugh, he saw the gleam of humor in her eye. "Very well. I accept your invitation on behalf of myself and my sister. Thank you."

"Oh, one thing more, before I take my leave of you."

She had the grace not to appear impatient with him. "Yes, Mr. Bolton?"

He took the half step necessary to bring him close enough to reach out, his hand going to the little white feather above her left ear, removing it carefully from her hair. "You've lost a feather."

Matilda's lips parted in surprise, her eyes widened as she took in the fluffy white plume. "Has that been there this whole time?" she asked, the last word coming out as more of a squeak.

His lips twitched as she raised her hand to accept the feather. "Never fear, Miss Rayment. You were perfectly intimidating and stern, even with the bit of fluff." He bowed, feeling cheeky, and hastily made his exit.

He hadn't seen Beatrice, but Oliver left encouraged just the same. Robert Dunwilde kept a box at the theater. All Oliver had to do was ask to accompany his friend, and the thing would be done.

Spending a single evening in Beatrice's company had once been a dream, but if he took the opportunity to court her, who knew what his future might entail? With Beatrice's sister seemingly no longer against the match, perhaps he finally had a chance.

CHAPTER 4

"*Y*ou did *what?*" Lady Granthorne asked, her voice rising dangerously. "Beatrice absolutely will *not* attend the theater with that young man, however charming he may be."

"Mother, please." Mattie stepped to the door of her mother's bedroom and closed it with haste. "Beatrice isn't going with him. She will not even know about the outing because *you* will make certain she is engaged elsewhere."

Her mother, dressed for the evening at Almack's, stood in stiff elegance beside her dressing table. "And where would that be? I cannot conjure invitations out of thin air." Her mother waved her hand about her head before rubbing at her temple.

"The Redhurst house party," Mattie said, unrepentant. "You were to leave Saturday morning. If we are clever, we can come up with an excuse for you going the evening before."

"I suppose that might work," her mother said, her brows drawing down in thought. "And their country house is only fifteen miles from London. That isn't a terrible distance, should your father need us."

Mattie clasped her gloved hands before her and considered the situation. "And we have already decided I would remain behind. So long as you return for the ball next Wednesday, you will not miss anything of importance in London. I can make our usual calls by myself."

Her mother closed her eyes tightly. "I do worry for your father."

"The staff will help, and I will be here as much as possible." Mattie went to her mother's side to take up the older woman's hands, fixing her with an earnest stare. "All will be well, Mother. Once Beatrice is taken care of, we can retire to the country to help Papa."

Lady Granthorne nodded, her expression unchanging. She returned Mattie's warm clasp, and her eyes grew distant. "If only we hadn't lost David."

It took all of Mattie's strength not to flinch at the name of her little brother, who had been between Mattie and Beatrice in age. He'd been gone twenty years, and her mother rarely mentioned him now. A childhood fever had stolen David, their father's heir, and the family had never quite been the same. If David had lived to adulthood, all manner of things would be different for the family.

"I know, Mama." Mattie kissed her mother's forehead. There had been a time when she wondered if her parents would've rather lost a daughter than the son, but they had loved her and Beatrice with their whole hearts. What parent would choose to lose *any* of their children? "I think about David all the time."

Mother's smile turned bittersweet. "I often wonder what he might have been like, as a grown gentleman. Thank Heaven for you and your sister. I do not know that I would have recovered without the two of you." Mother put her hand on Mattie's cheek, her eyes glistening with unshed tears. "My Mattie. We certainly asked a lot of you, as our oldest child. Sometimes, I worry it made you grow up too quickly."

Mattie grinned in an effort to lighten the moment. "I think I am naturally tyrannical. That is what you are trying to say, is it not? I am forever telling others what to do."

Mother chuckled. "If you were a sillier girl, or weren't so good at taking charge, I might've put a stop to things. But you are exceptionally clever and confident. I only hope such character traits continue to serve you."

Mattie pretended to preen, making her mother laugh again. Then she leaned down to take her mother's hand. "Come, Mama. Let us try and be cheerful this evening. There is much to do. And we are going to Almack's," Mattie said, whispering the last word as though it were a magic spell to cast out her mother's gloom.

By the time Mattie led the way into the sparkling ballroom, chandeliers glimmering and their light reflecting off the multitude of mirrors, Mother had regained her cheer. Beatrice followed them both with her usual grace and a roving eye that took in all the gentlemen present.

Mattie, paying careful attention to her sister, dropped back a step to link her arm through Beatrice's. "Do you see Mr. Redhurst? He asked for two dances with you this evening, did he not?"

"Hm? Oh, yes. Mr. Redhurst." Beatrice narrowed her eyes and looked around more carefully. After several moments of stretching about, Beatrice lifted a gloved hand to wave across the room at the one man who showed the most interest in her. "Here, he is coming to join us."

"Lovely." Mattie watched her sister's reaction to the

man's approach, attempting to discern how much work she must do to remove Oliver Bolton from Beatrice's thoughts. Given her sister's somewhat changeable nature, she hoped it would not be an enormous undertaking.

Beatrice's bright blue eyes widened happily, and she lowered her chin almost demurely when Mr. Redhurst arrived at her side.

He was a handsome man, six years Beatrice's senior, with sandy-colored hair and eyes a few shades darker than Beatrice's. Their children would likely be beautiful, given the attractiveness of the parents.

Nothing in Beatrice's manner indicated a change of feeling for Mr. Redhurst, which eased Mattie's mind somewhat. After an exchange of polite greetings with Mattie, Mr. Redhurst swept her younger sister away for a dance.

Mattie waited patiently for Beatrice's first dance to end, her eyes as often on the crowd around them as on Beatrice. Mr. Redhurst always asked Mattie to stand up with him at least once, which she counted in his favor. The man was incredibly thoughtful.

Mr. Redhurst's mother approached Mattie. "Good evening, Miss Rayment."

"Good evening, Mrs. Redhurst." Mattie curtsied to the lovely woman with all deference. "I am very glad to see you."

"As I am to see you." Mrs. Redhurst glanced briefly at the dancers, then back to Mattie. "You do not dance, Miss Rayment?"

"Not very often, I am afraid. Your son is always good enough to stand up with me for a dance. He is such a kind man." It wouldn't hurt to give a little flattery to the mother, Mattie well knew. "Beatrice often speaks of him with great regard."

"Indeed. My son speaks highly of your sister too." Mrs. Redhurst snapped her fan open and looked about them before she leaned closer to Mattie. "Your sister is a delightful girl, and the very sort I've always hoped he might find interest in."

Hardly believing her good luck, Mattie leaned closer to the matron to speak in a conspiratorial whisper. "Beatrice knows her good fortune, my dear Mrs. Redhurst. She has spoken of your house party with great excitement. I know she wishes she might be there as soon as possible, to see your beautiful home. My father may need the carriage Saturday morning," Mattie said, improvising and hoping the falsehood was not too terrible. "Beatrice is most distressed this may delay her arrival until Sunday."

Mrs. Redhurst turned fully to Mattie, her attitude one of accommodation. "That simply will not do. We have all manner of entertainments planned. Might it be better if your mother and sister came on Friday?" She glanced again at the whirling couples changing hands and places on the dance floor. "Then I might provide them both with a proper tour of the estate." There was no need to add the understanding that Mr. Redhurst would be present on that tour, giving the couple some much-needed time in each other's company.

"I believe that would do perfectly," Mattie said, holding her breath as she said the last word. Could it be so easy to slip her sister away before Oliver's evening at the theater? The invitation had practically fallen into her lap. Though she felt a sting of conscience for Oliver's sake. He would be terribly disappointed.

"Hm." Mrs. Redhurst raised her eyebrows. "I will speak with your mother."

"I am certain she will appreciate your generous offer, Mrs. Redhurst." Mattie took out her own fan and waved it languidly, putting on her most confident mask. "Mother is just there, across from the orchestra's perch, if you wish to speak to her now."

Mrs. Redhurst took her leave, making for Mattie's mother at once.

Now all Mattie had to worry about was breaking the news of Beatrice's absence to Oliver, who truly didn't deserve whatever painful feelings such a thing would cause. Mattie bit her bottom lip and wandered away to stand near the walls, making eye contact with herself in one of the gilded mirrors.

It's for the best. Beatrice would never be happy with Oliver, and that would make his life miserable. It was not that her sister was a terrible person, or a shrew, or immoral. Beatrice simply did not pay as much attention to the thoughts and feelings of others as most would consider prudent. Even if she felt true regard for Oliver Bolton, that feeling was unlikely to last when he denied her use of a carriage in order to spare horses for something else, or didn't purchase a bauble she would only wear once in order to buy something their estate actually needed. Beatrice didn't trouble herself over domestic affairs.

The memory of Beatrice and Oliver at the card party returned, and Mattie couldn't help thinking on Oliver's cheerful countenance. He'd thought himself lucky to be near Beatrice, and he hadn't bothered hiding it. A man who wore his affection so openly held little chance in reading Beatrice's many shifts in mind and mood.

Who knew her sister better than Mattie? No one. And she knew enough about Oliver's good heart and hard work to want to spare him the difficulties her sister would cause in his life. Mattie would handle him gently, guiding him as well as she could from disappointment to acceptance of the situation.

On the edge of the ballroom, Mattie quietly went through her plan, assuring herself she had done the right thing.

CHAPTER 5

*J*t took all Mattie's abilities to remain composed when Oliver Bolton called Friday evening. Though she'd rehearsed what she must say enough times to put even the most sophisticated actress to shame, her stomach writhed inside her. While she saw little choice in what must be done for Beatrice's security and Oliver's happiness, Mattie had never felt easy when telling a falsehood.

She paced the parlor, lit only by the fire and two candelabra's in opposite corners, wringing her hands enough that she worried over the seams of her gloves.

Oliver would be hurt. There was no question of that. His pride wounded, his pocket lighter for the purchase of theater tickets, and perhaps even others who would know of his plans and thus see his disappointment.

It was with that thought in mind, and the desire to spare him at least a little pain, that Mattie dressed herself for the theater. She could offer to attend with him. To help him save face in front of others, or to keep him company if he faced the evening before him on his own.

Not that he would accept such an offer. At least, she didn't let herself believe Oliver would agree to her company. Not when he wanted Beatrice's. But with her heart swimming in guilt, she had to at least offer some sort of olive branch to him.

Mattie and Mrs. Clifton, her mother's old friend and the chaperone for the evening, were waiting in the parlor. Mrs. Clifton, an elderly and genteel woman, had already dozed off in her seat near the fire when the butler showed Oliver into the room.

Mattie stood and curled her fingers tightly, watching as Oliver's eyes darted around the room, searching for Beatrice. Finally, his eyes settled on her, suspicious and a touch disappointed.

"Good evening, Mr. Bolton." She offered the customary curtsy to his bow. "I am afraid I have rather dreadful news."

He raised a hand, forestalling her explanation, his eyes crackling with indignation. "Your sister will not accompany me to the play." He turned away, the lines of his body stiff. "You might've at least sent word and spared me the humiliation of coming to your home."

Mattie's compassion for him pricked at her heart, but she could not remove her duty to her sister and her family. Mattie stepped closer, the silk of her evening gown swishing softly with each movement. "Mr. Bolton, please, it was not my intention to upset you." Indeed. She would spare him disappointment and pain, if she could. "Beatrice is not here, it is true, but when she returns you may spend time with her. She did not have a choice but to go, you see, as my mother insisted upon it only this morning."

She spoke quickly over the lie, relieved he didn't study her too closely. It would be harder to bear up the falsehood under any scrutiny. She hadn't sent a card to avoid him sending a response or appearing in person to wish Beatrice a safe journey.

"I thought to send round a card, but my day was taken up with helping the others pack, and then I decided it might be best to explain to you in person. They were to go to a house party tomorrow but were unexpectedly asked to arrive a day earlier."

Mattie took the last step between them and tilted her head, trying to peer up into his expression. "I am trying to handle the matter delicately, Mr. Bolton. Will you please forgive my bumbling attempts this once?"

Oliver spared her a sideways glance, brows drawn down, before he nodded. "I suppose I must." He put a hand to his cravat and smoothed the crisp white fabric in a gesture which could ruin the elaborate cascade of folds.

Mattie raised a hand to still his motion, but quickly pulled it back. The swift movement gained his attention, and he stared at her, eyebrows raised.

"I beg your pardon," she said, tucking the offending hand behind her back. "I am sorry for the disappointment. I wonder, Mr. Bolton, if you might still wish to attend the theater? I am dressed for it, you see. And there is Mrs. Clifton to chaperone. We might still have an enjoyable evening, though I know I am a poor substitute for Beatrice."

Those words settled heavily in Mattie's heart. Beatrice was prettier, livelier, and certainly better company than Mattie at social engagements. Most of the time, Mattie had too much on her mind to give herself up to the pleasures of society. Planning for Mr. Bolton to excuse her, the most likely thing to happen, made dressing for an evening out a less joyful affair than it otherwise might've been.

Oliver lifted his head and regarded her with a critical eye

before speaking. "You would still be willing to accompany me to the theater?"

"Why, yes," she stammered, taken aback by the intensity of his stare. "It hardly seems fair for you to give up the enjoyment and make the trouble of obtaining tickets a waste of time. I understand if you do not wish for my company—"

"Not at all," he said, his words clipped. "Although I had hoped to attend with both of the Miss Rayments, I would hardly be a gentleman to retract my invitation. I have a friend with a box, and he is expecting us." Oliver had the good manners to smile kindly at her, though she noted the look did not quite reach his eyes. They had been friends, of a sort. Maybe that remembrance kept him from crying off for the evening.

That he was still willing to take *her* with him, despite his disappointment in the evening, said something of his nature. She shouldn't have been surprised, yet she stood still for a moment, the prospect of going to the theater with him lifting her heart. It fell again nearly as quickly.

Truly, it almost made her feel worse about the whole ruse. Yet the invitation remained, and she had dressed for the theater.

"I will accompany you, Mr. Bolton, with the greatest pleasure. Allow me to—erm—bestir Mrs. Clifton." She hurried to rouse her chaperone, privately thinking it ridiculous her mother insisted she have one. After all, at twenty-six and with no plans for marrying, Mattie hardly thought it necessary. But even a spinster's reputation must be guarded.

It was almost insulting Matilda thought him simple enough to believe her story. Oliver may not have been a Cambridge or Oxford scholar, but he had a good head on his shoulders and sufficient instincts to know when someone lied to him. Although he suspected Matilda's motives were not cruel, after their last meeting he had genuinely thought she would give him an opportunity to prove his worthiness to her sister, her family, and Society as a whole.

While leaving her at home would have been the more satisfying response to her charade, he had made a fool of himself to Dunwilde and his other acquaintances by speaking of the evening with delighted anticipation. To arrive at the theater alone would be almost as terrible as not going at all.

The new world he inhabited put too much emphasis on one's social standing for him to ignore the rules of good manners.

Perhaps spending an evening with Matilda would prove educational. Observing her behavior during conversation would be enlightening. The first thing he must try to learn, of course, was whether or not Beatrice had even been aware that he had requested her company for the evening.

When they arrived at the theater, they went immediately to Dunwilde's box, where the man was sitting with a lady and the lady's mother. All rose to make their bows when Oliver presented Matilda.

"Miss Rayment, daughter of Baron Granthorne, and her companion, Mrs. Clifton."

"A pleasure, Miss Rayment," the young woman's mother said with a beaming smile. "And Mrs. Clifton. Come, you must sit next to me. We will let the young people sit at the front. Heaven knows, I have seen more than my share of plays."

Oliver showed Matilda to a chair and took his next to her. Next to him sat Robert Dunwilde and the young lady he escorted on the other side.

His friend wasted no time in leaning close to whisper. "I thought it was the younger sister you were interested in?"

Matilda stiffened in her chair and leaned forward, eyes intent upon the still-lowered curtain.

Oliver winced. Dunwilde had never been particularly good at whispering. And although his current situation was frustrating, he didn't wish to cause any offense.

"She was indisposed," Oliver answered quietly. "I am grateful Miss Rayment was still able to attend this evening."

The skeptical tilt to his friend's eyebrows said it all, and then the curtain was rising and half the room turned to the stage. The other half continued to examine members of the audience and gossip between chairs as well as between boxes.

Matilda was one of the few in attendance more interested in the stage than her neighbors. Oliver studied his opponent as covertly as possible. He knew, somehow, that he had been put in an awkward position on purpose. The lovely Matilda Rayment had never meant for him to escort her sister anywhere at all. What remained to be seen was how far she might be willing to go, what manner of tricks she might enact, to keep him distanced from Beatrice.

Appealing to the parents would do him no favors, either. The baron and baroness would most likely scoff at him for entertaining such notions as courting their younger daughter.

But if he could convince Matilda, perhaps she could persuade their parents to treat him with fairness instead of snobbery.

After all, as a landed gentleman—even if the land wasn't

yet as successful as it could be — he was an appropriate choice for a suitor.

While the actors sang of love on stage, Oliver mentally prepared to do battle to win the right to court whom he wished.

CHAPTER 6

*M*attie sat in her father's library, reading aloud while her father drew. His lucid moments, his ability to converse like himself, became rarer with each passing week. But if his hands were busy, he was often capable of maintaining greater focus on the world around him.

Though the reading wasn't exactly required, Matilda found it necessary in order to keep her mind from turning continually to the rather dishonorable lies she'd told Oliver. He'd hardly said a word all the night long, during the opera and after, though he'd been a complete gentleman.

Her voice faltered as she read, the dry text closing up her throat completely.

"Something wrong, Mattie girl?" her father asked, glancing up briefly from his sketch. "You aren't your usual lively self today."

When was the last time she'd even thought to apply the term *lively* to herself or any of her pursuits?

"No, Papa. I apologize for my distraction. Shall I continue reading?"

"You needn't. I am finished with your likeness." He handed her the folder wherein he kept his sketches, and she took it, curious despite herself. Sometimes he drew her as a child, nearly perfect representations of what she'd looked like when she was young.

Today's drawing was of her reading a book, her brow furrowed and her eyes dark with thought. She swallowed at the sight of her guilt, captured quite innocently by her father.

"You appear...concerned," her father said, his gaze gentle. "Is something troubling you, my dear?"

She stared into his eyes, remembering all the childhood woes she used to bring to him. He would put her on his knee and listen, intent on her every word, and then put her world to rights. If only he could do that for her now.

"At times I wonder at my choices," she said softly, not looking away, hoping her father stayed in the present with her instead of drifting away to the past. "I try to do the right thing, not only for myself but for others."

"That is an admirable trait, my dear. Do you know, I will never forget when that boy came to live with our steward. You fretted and worried over how lonely he must be. Do you remember? Until you finally scrounged up the courage to go and speak to him and tell him how sorry you were for his loss."

Her throat closed up, making it hard for her to get her words out past the lump. "You remember that?"

"Of course I do. I was so proud of you. The grief of others can be a frightening thing to face. I think in part because it is human nature to avoid grief, whatever the cost. Yet grief is as much a part of life as joy." He took up her hand and gave it a squeeze.

Mattie almost confessed to him then. He seemed so much

himself. If she could only lay her troubles at his feet, as she used to, and have him pull the pieces together again with her, things would be so much better.

"Will your mother and sister be joining us this evening?" he asked, looking to the door and back to her.

Mattie's heart fell. She had already told him, twice, that they were away for a few days. She couldn't tell him of her woes. Not anymore. They were as likely to distress him and send him deeper into the fog as anything else.

A knock at the door gave her leave to turn her attention away from the troubling image.

"Come in, please," she said.

A footman opened the door, and a maid came in, carrying a very large basket stuffed with every sort of flower imaginable.

Mattie rose. "Oh, dear. Beatrice would have loved these. We must endeavor to keep them fresh for her." She came to the maid, her hands outstretched to examine the blossoms.

"They aren't for your sister, Miss Rayment," the maid said, delight coloring her tone. "They're for you. There's a card."

"For me?" Mattie saw the card held by the footman and took it with murmured thanks.

Miss Matilda Rayment,

Thank you for sparing my feelings and enjoying the theater with me. I hope I might extend another invitation to you, in the name of friendship, to ride with me in the park today. Please send your acceptance to the address enclosed. If you must send your regrets, I will strive to understand. But it is good to be around familiar people in a city full of strangers.

Yours, etc.,

O. Bolton

MATTIE STARED AT THE NOTE, THE LITTLE LINES AND LETTERS jumbled about in her head; when she finally made sense of them, she could hardly believe it.

"Oliver Bolton has invited me to ride in the park today," she said, sparing a moment of pride that the sentence came out evenly.

"Mr. Hapsbury's nephew?" her father said, and she turned to him in shock. He sometimes forgot she was a woman of six and twenty instead of merely sixteen, but he could remember the name of the orphaned boy?

"Yes. The very same."

"Always liked that boy. Full of ambition, and a hard worker." Father chewed at the insides of his cheeks for a moment, his eyebrows drawing down. "We ought to have him to dinner if he is in town. Invite him while you are on your ride today, Mattie girl."

A direct order, issued when his thoughts were clear, must be obeyed. But—she was trying to rid the family of Oliver's intentions, not bring him more fully into the fold.

"Then you do not object to my riding with him?" she asked carefully, folding the card and running her index finger over the crease.

"Not in the least." Her father settled himself more comfortably into the couch and took up his drawing again. The footman still held the door and the maid still held the basket of flowers. They both appeared overly interested in her answer. Mattie took in their expressions, noting the maid's anticipation with distress.

Astounding as it may be that a man would send her a

bouquet, servants ought to be more circumspect. It was not as if this outing would be anything but cordial.

Mattie sighed and took in the riotous blossoms again, trying to remember when she'd last received flowers from a gentleman. It had been *years*.

"Put these in the entry, Sarah, and inform the groom I will need my horse at a quarter till five." Mattie tucked the card into the ribbon at her waist and went back to sit next to her father, picking up the book again and effectively dismissing the servants with their curious stares.

"I am glad to see a young man take notice of you," her father said, not looking up from his work. "You are a good girl, and I want you to be happy, Mattie."

Nervous laughter bubbled up inside her. "Mr. Bolton is but a friend, Papa. I am too old to be of interest to anyone. I'm content to be here with you and Mama." She looked down at the book in her hands, not really seeing it and uncertain as to where she'd left off reading.

Her father sighed and shook his head, but he said nothing more, leaving Mattie to her thoughts and suppositions of what Oliver Bolton could mean by sending her *flowers*.

Perhaps he had decided to court her favor, in the hopes of winning Beatrice's interest. That made the most sense of any of her musings. Most assumed the sisters had a close relationship, and they were not exactly wrong. Mattie would do anything for her sister, but she knew her approval or disapproval never swayed Beatrice's mind. That was why she had to concentrate her efforts on Oliver, rather than her sister, to see to it they were kept apart until Mr. Redhurst secured Beatrice's hand.

But, a hopeful little corner of her heart insisted, wouldn't it be lovely if Oliver's note was sincere? A friendship with someone like him, though all she would ever receive, would be most lovely.

CHAPTER 7

*O*liver clutched Matilda's acceptance in his hand with something near to triumph. Either she was oblivious to his motives or else curious to see what he could want with her. No matter the reason, she had agreed to spend more time in his presence, which meant he had greater opportunity to present his himself as an acceptable suitor.

As a youth, Miss Beatrice's tinkling laughs and witty remarks enchanted him. Now that he'd inherited, he finally had a way to enjoy the pleasure of her company, and he would not allow it to be taken from him so swiftly. If he had to win approval from Matilda Rayment first, then so be it.

Five o'clock found him at the baron's home, with Matilda already mounted on a fine chestnut gelding, wearing a smart hazel riding habit that suited her coloring. Her cheeks were rosy and her smile easier than he had seen it so far.

"You do realize," she said after they'd greeted one another, "that Rotten Row will not afford much of an actual *ride* at this time of day? We will spend most of our time weaving in and out of carriages or standing still."

"You do not seem concerned over such a fate," he returned, not having to remind himself to be pleasant. The day was lovely, and Matilda was in a friendly mood. They took to the road, each mounted atop their own horse, and followed a slow line of carriages and horsemen moving in the direction of Hyde Park.

"I am merely happy to be in the fresh air with good company," she stated firmly.

"A kind compliment, Miss Rayment." If Matilda thought him good company, perhaps convincing her to allow him to court Beatrice would prove easier than he thought.

She raised her eyebrows. "How do you know I meant you? I could've been talking of my horse."

For a startled moment, Oliver wasn't sure what to say, but when he saw the pink in her cheeks and her upturned lips, he started to smile. "Ah, I see. Naturally, a horse is a fine companion, especially when one intends to ride."

Matilda's shoulders noticeably relaxed, and she gave him a brighter smile. "I haven't ridden through the park in some time, Mr. Bolton. Nor has my friend Coriander."

Oliver chuckled and nudged his horse to ride alongside her. "You named your horse after a spice?"

"I name all my animals after spices. I made a sort of traditional theme of it after naming our childhood kitten. Do you not remember him?"

"Basil," he said, the little black ball of fluff coming abruptly into his memory. "I rescued that loathsome creature from the eaves of a window once. How could I forget him?" He'd had to borrow a ladder from the gardener and regretted not borrowing a sturdy pair of gloves as well when the kitten unleashed its tiny, razor-like claws upon him.

Matilda had thanked him profusely, while the cat tucked

in her arms glared at him, and she had offered to bandage up his hands.

She seemed to be remembering the same event. "Have you any lasting scars from that encounter?"

Oliver looked down at the leather gloves he wore now, smooth and supple, the gloves of a gentleman instead of a gardener. How strange, the difference a few years could make in one's circumstances. "I think not. I healed tolerably well. What of the cat?"

"He has grown quite portly and spends his days sleeping in warm patches of sunlight and giving Cook grief," she answered, a lilt in her voice as she spoke. "He is a most abominable creature, but I do adore him."

They gave attention to the road for a time, weaving around ambling carriages, and then they were on the paths of Hyde Park. Riding abreast was less comfortable, if they wished to avoid collision with other riders or fine little vehicles with shiny wheels and tall seats. Oliver tipped his hat to every woman they passed, earning a few smiles and nods in return. Matilda made her share of greetings, calling out names when she knew them, but never stopping to speak to anyone.

When the opportunity presented itself, he urged his horse forward to her side once more. "Have you no wish to socialize today, Miss Rayment?"

She looked askance at him. "Did you have someone you wished to speak to, Mr. Bolton?"

"I am afraid my circle of acquaintances is quite small," he admitted, looking around the path. "I have seen no one I know."

She drew up her horse. "Oh. I beg your pardon. Might I introduce you to anyone? I know several of the people we've passed. I am sorry, I wasn't thinking—"

Oliver waved the apology aside without concern. "Perhaps another time." His horse slowed to a stop when the barouche in front of them halted. Oliver stood taller in the stirrups, trying to see over the crowd while his horse danced to the side.

"Have you not ridden through the park yet?" Matilda asked, and he turned to see her horse placidly bending to nibble at the grass near the path. "It is more standing still than it is moving, especially in our fine spring weather." She grinned at him from beneath the brim of her riding hat.

"I confess, I've heard that is the case, but I hoped such accounts were exaggerated."

Matilda didn't appear perturbed in the slightest. Her attention turned to the Serpentine, as they were as near its shores as one could get on Rotten Row.

"It isn't like at home," she said, her voice grown softer along with her expression. "One can have a good, brisk ride and suitable exercise without worrying if anyone notices your new hat."

"Should I have said something about your hat?" he asked, wondering where her melancholy air came from. "I am afraid the expectations of Society are yet new to me."

Matilda's attention redirected to him, her eyebrows raised. "You ought not make such comments, Mr. Bolton. You are a gentleman, and you need make no excuses. In all honesty, you comport yourself as well as any lord I have come across."

The vehicle ahead of them moved, necessitating that they both continue forward, giving Oliver a moment to think on what she said. The woman barely knew him. How could she hold such an opinion of his character already?

"But you really should say something kind about a lady's riding cap. Especially when it has pheasant feathers smartly applied to the brim instead of haphazardly placed in her curls." One side of her mouth quirked upward, and Oliver had to chuckle as she tossed her head, the better to show off the headpiece.

"Forgive me, Miss Rayment. Your feathers are most becoming today." They were passing a carriage going the opposite direction, and the woman inside gave him a most peculiar look for that comment. "And very well placed."

"That is much better. Thank you." She bestowed a deep nod upon him, but as she faced forward, that wistful sort of expression came into her eyes again. "Your uncle would be proud you've adjusted to the manners of a gentleman so well. I look forward to giving him a firsthand account of your time in London."

Oliver had written to his uncle weekly since inheriting the Lincolnshire estate, asking advice, bemoaning the rundown house and flooded fields, and finally, in the last eighteen months, sharing all that had finally gone *right* with the estate.

"I didn't expect he would tell the whole neighborhood when I wrote, but he must've for you to be knowledgeable of my work," Oliver said. "My uncle is not usually known for being talkative." He turned to share a humorous smile with Matilda, but she turned her eyes downward and fiddled with her reins as they drew to another stop. "Is something troubling you, Miss Rayment?"

"No. Not at all." Quite abruptly, she lifted her chin and fixed him with a curious look. "You haven't been in London long. Have you visited the Royal menagerie yet? Or any of the art galleries? Will you be attending services while you are in town?"

Oliver's mind puzzled over her abrupt change in topic, but he answered easily enough. "I have seen very little and done very little. I had hoped my friend, Mr. Dunwilde, would guide me for a time, but he's left on a shooting trip in the country. I suppose," he added with what he hoped was carelessness, lowering his gaze, "I must find my own way." Something he'd been doing a lot of the past five years.

Her tone of voice when she spoke, in a rushed manner, was perfectly sympathetic. "Oh dear, but that isn't done. You must be introduced into the correct circles, if you mean to make a place for yourself in society. Especially if you wish to court Beatrice."

The name being mentioned so suddenly startled Oliver out of his thoughts. Miss Beatrice. Of course. Somehow Oliver had completely forgotten about the purpose of this ride—to show Mattie that he was a proper fit for Beatrice. "Your sister enjoys her place in Society a great deal, doesn't she?" he asked, moving forward again in the line of carriages. "I imagine she is popular."

"Her company has been sought after by many in years past. And she did leave for that house party rather hastily." Matilda didn't look at him as she spoke, though her manner became less animated. "She is not a retiring sort of person. Beatrice enjoys being at the center of grand events."

"I cannot think how many of those I might be invited to attend," Oliver said slowly, his eyes on the horizon. Could he change that, somehow? He had never found making new acquaintances an easy task.

They were moving again, coming to the end of Rotten Row.

"Once people know you, they will count themselves lucky to have you at their parties and balls." Matilda cast him a genuine smile. "I have always found you to be pleasant company, after all."

He chuckled, feeling somewhat grateful for the comment

despite from who offered it. The fact did not escape him that she had now mentioned the pleasure of his company not once, but twice. It caused him to wonder. "We did not exactly spend a great deal of time in each other's company, Miss Rayment." He could only remember a handful of their interactions, though they had lived in the same village for six years. He was forever about on his uncle's business, which was truly estate business for the baron's family, and Matilda was being molded into a proper lady along with her younger sister.

"What about that time in the study, during that terrible storm? Do you remember?" she asked, turning her horse onto the street. "It had been raining for ages and ages. Your uncle sent you to the library for a book, I think."

For several seconds, Oliver felt certain she was mistaken in her memory, but then he began to recall such an afternoon. "I didn't know you were in the library, hiding behind the curtain."

She wrinkled her nose at him. "I wasn't *hiding*. I was sitting on the window seat."

"Behind the curtain." He narrowed his eyes at her.

"Halfway behind the curtain, perhaps," she returned, pursing her lips.

Oliver chuckled. "I know enough to refrain from contradicting a lady. Yes. I remember. You were on the window seat, and I came in looking for the book, and there was that monstrous burst of lightning—"

"And you screamed," she interrupted with barely concealed glee. "Or shrieked, more like. I didn't know *you* were there, so that frightened me, and I fell out of the window seat."

Which had made the curtains fly open—and she had hit the ground with a shockingly loud thump. He started to laugh, remembering how he'd lifted the book in his hands like a weapon only to see Matilda crawling out from under the drapes, hair in disarray and face frozen in shock. They had both stared at each other, he with raised book and she from her hands and knees on the ground.

Matilda started laughing too, covering her mouth with a gloved hand when a matron riding by sent a withering glance their direction.

"I thought you said I was good company? Nothing about that scene strikes me as evidence of that." Oliver couldn't keep the amusement from his voice, though he tried to compose himself, with poor results.

"You don't remember?" she asked, tipping her head to one side. "You dropped the book on the floor and rushed to help me to my feet." She grinned at him. "Quite the gentleman, really, considering you were as frightened as I was."

"How old were we?" he asked, furrowing his brow in thought. "Thirteen?"

"Near there, I should think. You hadn't started calling me Miss Rayment yet, but you'd been with us for a good while." She turned away, her profile lovely and expression soft. "You stayed in the library for at least a quarter of an hour, trying to soothe my nerves."

"Trying to soothe my own," he added. "It was a blow to my thirteen-year-old ego, to be so unmanned in the presence of a young lady over a crack of lightning." Missing his parents and trying to find a place for himself, Oliver hadn't possessed much confidence in those days. "I didn't want you running off to tell my uncle any tales, after all."

Matilda raised a gloved hand to her heart. "Me, sir? I would *never* do such a thing." She batted her eyelashes and put on an expression of innocence, making him grin. Their horses were nearing her house. "I thought you a very nice boy. Why would I make trouble for you?"

"You wouldn't, of course. But that was before I knew the family very well. I hadn't been acquired to assist with dancing or etiquette lessons. I was only my uncle's errand boy, and I had no wish to upset him. Poor Uncle Hapsbury. He hadn't any idea what to do with me most of the time."

Indeed, Oliver could remember several instances when his uncle had looked over the rims of his spectacles in a state of befuddlement, trying to sort out whether to laugh or scold Oliver over his misadventures.

"I think he did a marvelous job with you, overall," Matilda said, her tone sincere and her eyes meeting his squarely.

"Thank you." And then, because he was starting to feel guilty over enjoying Matilda's company, he added, "I hope Miss Beatrice feels the same."

Matilda's approving look vanished, replaced by a more distant, polite expression. Perhaps she had forgotten his purpose in regards to Beatrice, too. They were at her house again, and a servant appeared at the door to take her horse. Matilda dismounted and turned her attention to him. "Thank you for the enjoyable afternoon, Mr. Bolton."

He dismounted as well and stepped forward, feeling an apology was in order but uncertain *what* he was apologizing for. "Miss Rayment, I—"

The front door flung open, crashing against the wall and interrupting his words, and her father came hurrying down the steps.

"Mattie," he said, sounding breathless. A male servant followed close at his heels, eyes wide and face pale. "Mattie, I cannot find your mother, or your sister. Where have you been?" He was obviously agitated as he reached for his daughter, enfolding her in his arms upon the walk.

Matilda's face paled as she accepted the embrace, and she appeared dreadfully off balance. Her father had sounded near to tears, and his size easily overwhelmed her smaller frame.

Oliver handed his reins to the groom. There were few other people around, but Oliver could sense something of a scene building.

"My lord," he said, giving his attention to the baron. "I am afraid I kept your daughter out too long. We went for a ride in Hyde Park."

"Yes, Papa. You see. Here I am." Matilda turned an apologetic eye to Oliver. "And Mother and Beatrice are well. Come inside, and I will tell you everything."

The baron looked around the street, then at Oliver, before he loosened his grip on his daughter's arms. "Won't you come inside too, young man?" he said, eyebrows drawn down in puzzlement, as though he could not remember Oliver's name. The fear had left his voice, all at once, though evidence of tears remained upon the man's cheeks.

Matilda's eyes widened, and she looked at Oliver in something of a panic. "Mr. Bolton likely has other demands on his time, Papa."

Oliver's shoulders dropped, and he looked from the horses, still standing in the grip of the young servant, around the street, where there were now several pairs of curious eyes watching their little tableau.

He lowered his voice so only Matilda and her father might hear. "I would very much like to come in, Miss Rayment, and you needn't fear. I am not wholly unaware of your circumstances, and I am a man of discretion." Though he hadn't realized things were quite this bad. He had thought, since the baron had come to London, the man might have improved.

Understanding lit her face. "Your uncle's letters?"

He doffed his hat. "Won't you lead the way, my lord?"

The baron's confusion cleared, and he stood straighter, more like his old self. "Yes, of course. Come. We must go inside." He walked before them, forgetting to take his daughter's arm. Oliver moved to offer his, and they followed the baron—and the servant who had hovered at the edge of the conversation—into the townhouse.

CHAPTER 8

*M*attie made certain her father was comfortably settled in his favorite chair in the study, going to the trouble of giving him an extra cushion and a warm shawl around his shoulders. She tried to ignore Oliver, who stood by the window, staring out to the street. She bustled around the room to stoke the fire, rang for refreshments, found her father a book, and then stood for a moment in uncertainty.

Mr. Hapsbury, their steward, was not a gossip. In fact, the man had been a loyal employee to her father since before Mattie's birth. But he had obviously told Oliver something of her father's ailment.

I cannot be entirely surprised, given how much he's told me of Oliver's accomplishments.

Mattie reached up to touch her hair and realized she still wore her riding cap. Grimacing, she began to undo the pins which held the lovely thing in place. Once it was removed, she laid it aside on a table.

Oliver's hands were clasped behind his back, and she couldn't see his face. It was impossible to guess what he thought of the situation, though he had acted quickly to help move everyone into the house to minimize what onlookers saw.

Father must've been watching at the window for her or the other ladies of the house to arrive home. His state had been one of worry and agitation. Thankfully, the agitation hadn't lasted long. Again, she questioned the wisdom of their father coming with them for the Season, though they intended to stay only so long as it took to secure Beatrice a marriage offer.

Her mother hadn't wanted to leave him on their estate, and Mattie really couldn't imagine doing so either.

Mattie said nothing as she approached Oliver. At first, before her courage built up suitably, she only gazed out the window alongside him. A carriage passed, and across the street a woman walked hand in hand with two little boys. Life continued as it always had.

"I didn't mean to intrude," Oliver said, startling her from her quiet study of the world outside the house, and outside her difficulties.

Mattie turned enough to see his cast-down expression, the frown pulling at his brow and mouth.

"I apologize if it made you uncomfortable," she answered softly. Beatrice was rarely ever near their father of late, claiming it unsettled her too much when he had one of his "fits," as she called them. Mattie knew most of society would feel similarly, and she didn't blame them. Sometimes it made her uncomfortable too. Mostly, it made her heart ache. To see her father like this was something she had never imagined she might experience. She glanced over at her father, who now sat in a comfortable chair turning over the pages of a book.

Oliver shook his head, still not facing her. "My uncle said

your father had been forgetful of late. There is more to it than that, isn't there?"

She swallowed and lowered her eyes to the ground, trying to put her words in order before she spoke. "He is forgetful, but it is not so small a thing as mislaying spectacles or a book. He is mislaying his recent memories and living in moments from the past. Some days, he speaks as though I am still a child. Other times it is like what you saw: he cannot remember what is going on about him and becomes afraid."

Oliver tipped his head in acknowledgement of what she said before asking, "What has the doctor said? I assume a doctor's been consulted."

"At home, yes. And Mother sought out the help of physicians here in London. None of them are hopeful of curing my father. They say it is the result of growing old, of melancholia." Mattie wrapped her arms around herself, wishing she could ward off the dread of the diagnosis. "They call it *mania mentalis*."

"As if naming it in Latin makes it better." Oliver looked sideways at her, and his eyes swirled with compassion and concern. "I am sorry for it, Matilda," he said, her Christian name slipping from his lips, sounding quite natural. Indeed, something in his tone of voice soothed her as a gentle touch might. "Your father is a good man, honorable and kind. If there is anything I might do to assist your family, please tell me."

The sincerity with which he spoke warmed her weary heart. "No one knows," she whispered. "Outside the family and a few of the servants. If people knew, if they guessed, we would be ostracized." It was yet another reason she had to secure Beatrice's happiness with haste, in order to withdraw from London.

No one wanted to marry into a family where such diseases of the mind were present. Even if there was no indication Mattie or Beatrice would ever suffer from the same.

Oliver regarded her silently for a moment before he nodded. "I will not speak of it to anyone, Miss Rayment."

"Is he staying for dinner?" her father asked loudly, causing both her and Oliver to start. They had been speaking in near whispers.

Mattie looked from her father's inquisitive face, peering around the side of his chair, up to Oliver's almost amused expression. He didn't look disgusted or distressed. He looked, she thought, rather the same as he had on their ride. Thoughtful, kind, and handsome.

"If you would like me to stay, sir, I will most happily. A bachelor takes his meals wherever he can." He cut a glance to her long enough to offer a smile and a wink, then he strode over to her father. "Won't you tell me of your home, my lord? It has been years since I've been for a visit, and I rather miss it."

Mattie watched, attempting to remain unemotional, as Oliver settled into a chair near her father and conversed as if the scene in the road had never occurred. As if everything were *normal*. Nothing had been normal for ages.

Her heart lurched inside her thinking of the task ahead. She wished her sister might return from the house party engaged to wed, before Oliver became too attached. Then Mattie would not have to be the one to dash this good man's hopes of courting Beatrice. She looked at him once more with her father, soaking in the sweetness of the scene. Sparing Oliver's feelings while diverting them from Beatrice would be challenging indeed.

CHAPTER 9

*O*liver allowed Matilda's father to guide their conversation, whether the baron spoke of things long past or occurring in the present. The man's grasp on time was loose, yet Oliver would never question his intelligence. While they spoke in the study, Oliver's eyes often strayed to Matilda. She remained near, though she did not participate in the conversation.

She wrote at the desk for a time, looking through what appeared to be a ledger, then took up a book and sat in a chair across the room from the gentlemen. She occasionally glanced in their direction and offered the faintest of smiles, then went back to her reading. The servant who had come out into the street, the baron's valet, came in and out of the room frequently, acting the part of a companion.

The family must've given the man additional duties when the baron's memory began to fail. No wonder Matilda had stayed behind when her mother and sister went to the house party in the country. It was obvious she stayed for her father more so than she had stayed for Oliver and their appointment to the theater.

This diminished his pride a touch. He'd fancied that she stayed merely to warn him away, but her duty to her father was more likely the reason for her continued presence in London.

"Mattie is a lovely girl, isn't she?" the baron said, startling Oliver from his thoughts. He realized he'd been staring at her again, while Matilda was tucked rather snuggly into the pages of her book and oblivious to the world around her.

What could he do but agree? "She is. You are very fortunate in your daughters." There. That was a good, general sort of compliment.

The baron pulled the shawl tighter around his thin shoulders. "She worries too much. Takes too much on herself." He spoke quietly, and Oliver noticed the baron's blue eyes were lucid and bright. "It isn't right for a young woman like her to worry so over her parents. She ought to have a husband and children of her own."

While Oliver had certainly been surprised to find Beatrice remained unwed, he hadn't given much thought to Matilda's situation. Now that the baron mentioned it, he found it strange no gentleman had offered for her. Matilda Rayment might not be the golden-haired beauty her sister was, but she had an allure of her own Oliver could not deny. Her dry sense of humor and the way she expressed herself with clarity and sincerity were qualities he rather liked.

And she did have striking eyes.

"Why hasn't she married?" Oliver asked, turning to face the baron again. Speaking of Matilda had naturally made his attention return to her corner of the room. "Surely there have been offers."

"There have. A few." The baron settled back into his chair and looked out the window, and Oliver wondered if that would be the end of the conversation, as it appeared the baron might lose the thread of the present again. "I think she's waiting for someone special to come along," the baron said at last.

Before Oliver could give much thought to that, the butler arrived, announcing dinner.

Matilda rose from her chair with an easy sort of grace. Most of the young women at the beginning of their time in society held themselves like statues, afraid to move in the wrong manner, but Matilda had confidence in her bearing.

"I hope you do not mind the informality of the occasion, Mr. Bolton," she said, coming nearer where he and her father sat.

"Nonsense." The baron chortled as he rose. "What young man *wants* to spend half an hour dressing like a dandy to take soup and bread? I lay odds that Oliver is happy to forgo the rituals of a formal evening."

"Oh, Papa." Matilda came forward and reached for her father's arm, but the gentleman swiftly raised it to fuss with the shawl around his shoulders.

"Ah, Oliver. Do a favor for your elder, and escort Mattie in to the table. Mattie, send Matthews to me, won't you?"

Oliver stepped in to offer Matilda his arm, noting the way her brows were drawn together in concern.

"I cannot think of a command I would be happier to obey, my lord," he said, affecting his most chivalrous grin.

Matilda smiled at him, taking his offered arm. "Papa, I will send your valet to you at once. But no tidying your cravat. It wouldn't be fair to Mr. Bolton."

Startled, Oliver tucked his chin down in order to inspect his cravat, prepared to see the crisp white cloth wrinkled beyond repair. But the *mathematique* arrangement looked nearly as fine as it had when he left his apartments to accompany Matilda on their ride.

The woman made a sound suspiciously like a giggle, which she turned into clearing her throat. "This way, Mr. Bolton." She gestured to the hall, and he guided her to the dining room.

He helped her to a chair near the head of the table near the head, then seated himself across from her. "How did you know about my difficulties with my cravat?"

Before answering his query, she directed a footman to send her father's valet to him. Lifting her glass rather primly, Matilda arched an eyebrow at him. "I recall your uncle constantly telling you to look to your neckwear. I think it was a nervous habit of yours, was it not, to tug at it?"

Oliver sat back in his chair. "You remember that?" And how many times had she been in his presence to witness such a thing? "That's rather astonishing, Miss Rayment, isn't it?"

Her cheeks colored. "Where could Papa have disappeared to?" she asked, leaning to look through the doorway they'd entered. Trusting to the informality of the evening, Oliver put an elbow on the table and rested his chin in his hand.

"Miss Matilda Rayment, you are avoiding my question. Why did you take notice of the nervous habits of a servant?"

"You weren't a servant," she said, studying the tablecloth. "Your uncle holds a respected position in our employment. Besides, other than Beatrice, you were the closest person to me in age for miles and miles."

"That's true. I am—what was it? Sixty-three days older than you?" She'd wasted no time in calculating that when they'd first met, after discovering they were the same age.

The baron entered the room, and Oliver realized their

private conversation must be cut short. He found he was far too interested in probing further into their shared past and her opinions of him.

"You haven't started without me, Mattie girl?"

"Never, Papa."

The baron took his seat at the head of the table, and the footmen moved to place platters of food upon the table.

Oliver gave his attention to Lord Granthorne. Dinner passed pleasantly, the three of them conversing on any subject the baron chose. Somehow, by the end of the evening, Oliver had agreed to accompany them both to Sunday services the next morning.

As he mounted his horse to leave, Oliver allowed himself to be pleased with the evening. He'd made a good impression on the baron, and Matilda seemed to be thawing towards him. Perhaps by the time Beatrice returned home with her mother, his company would be welcomed.

Of course, making his way through the streets of London, he realized he hadn't passed such a pleasant evening with good company in months. He didn't entertain much, as a bachelor, at Westerwind. His neighbors invited him to dine on occasion, but he had yet to feel like anything more than a dinner guest.

He couldn't think of one uncomfortable moment at the baron's table, nor could he recall any dinner companion being as intriguing as Matilda Rayment.

CHAPTER 10

*S*omehow, between the end of the Sunday sermon and reaching their carriage, Mattie's father had extended an invitation to Oliver for that very afternoon and coerced the young man into accepting. Really, it was almost unseemly to see Oliver three days in a row, in such intimate settings as the theater, the house, and church services. Now they would see each other twice within the same day.

If anyone had known, there would certainly be gossip as to what his intentions were regarding Mattie.

Mattie sat before her mirror as her maid finished tidying her hair. At least she didn't have to wonder about Oliver's motives for spending time in her company. Of course, it would be best if she stopped enjoying their conversations and instead showed him how wrong Beatrice was for him.

Catching her furrowed brow in the mirror, Mattie nearly groaned aloud.

She'd hardly done a thing to dissuade Oliver from her sister. Hadn't that been her plan? Wasn't it the wisest course of action?

Hopefully Beatrice would be engaged when she arrived

back in London, and there would be nothing more to worry about. Except, of course, Oliver's feelings. Would he be greatly injured if Beatrice announced her betrothal? Doubtless he would take pains to avoid the family, at least for a time.

The Season would soon be over when summer's heat intruded upon London's busy streets. Oliver would then return to his home in Lincolnshire. It might be another year before she saw him again, if her family even attempted to return to London. Much depended upon her father's health.

The thought pulled her up abruptly, halting her mind the way a dam halted a winding stream. It had been good to see Oliver, once she'd become used to his grown-up self, to speak to him and be in his company. Being with him brought back memories of happier, simpler days at their estate.

He'd been a tall and lanky boy the first time she saw him, and he'd only stretched out more as he grew. She'd been jealous of him the year they turned fourteen, telling him it wasn't fair he was half a head taller than she when he was only threescore days older.

"Are you eager to tower over all the men you dance with in London?" he'd asked, his voice cracking with his sense of humor. She'd huffed at him and walked away with all the dignity a girl of that age could possess.

Mattie smiled with the memory.

Her height, which was unremarkably average, didn't matter much anymore, as she was rarely asked to dance anyway. Unless a man was interested in Beatrice. It hadn't bothered her, as her lack of partners indicated everyone well knew her desire to remain unwed.

Beatrice had flirted her way about London from the first moment she'd stepped foot on its cobbled road, and she did so without any desire to keep one of her many catches as a husband. While Mattie had never been particularly interested in finding a husband either, her reasons were entirely different from her sister's. A husband would be inclined to tell her what to do, when she had a perfectly capable head on her shoulders. And she'd watched several young ladies of her acquaintance marry into less than favorable circumstances.

Oliver, a kind soul and conscientious landowner, would likely never give a wife cause to regret taking his name.

"I've never seen a man put a blush in your cheeks, miss."

Mattie started in her chair, meeting her maid's eyes in the mirror. She'd forgotten she wasn't alone, and her maid's comment took a moment to fully sink into her consciousness.

"I wasn't blushing," Mattie said, leaning forward to peer at her cheeks. "It is hot in the room." She bit her lip over the falsehood. Her windows faced east; the sun threw its heat into the opposite side of the house, leaving her room quite cool. Even if her cheeks were not.

"As you say, miss." Her maid bobbed a somewhat cheeky curtsy before withdrawing, as Mattie had thought she'd done several minutes before. The door shut quietly behind the servant, and Mattie glared at herself in the mirror.

"I *wasn't* blushing," she whispered firmly. "And certainly not over Ol—a man."

Sitting straighter, she spoke with determination. "My duties are to help Beatrice obtain a suitable match, care for Papa, and assist in running the family estate." She nodded to herself and stood from the table, ordering her thoughts.

After searching out her father, Mattie suggested they spend the afternoon in the gardens. The day was fine, for March, and fresh air would do everyone a great deal of good. Hopefully the outdoors could help her clear her head before Oliver arrived to pay his call. Mattie had arranged her father comfortably on the terrace while she clipped flowers for an arrangement. Mattie had just taken her gardening gloves off and put her blooms in a pail of water when she heard steps on the terrace.

"Good afternoon, my lord," Oliver said, making his bows. "Miss Rayment."

"There's a good lad, Oliver." Having one of his better days, the cordiality in the baron's voice was most sincere. Mattie, standing behind his bench, shared a smile with Oliver. "Tell me, have you been well since we last parted? Had any adventures?"

It was a question Mattie had heard many times in her life. Whenever she came in from play or saw her father at the end of a long day, he would ask her that very thing.

"None of which to speak, my lord. Though I wonder if your daughter might join me in a small one? The adventure of taking a turn about the garden. If you will excuse her?"

Their town garden wasn't particularly large, but it afforded enough space and greenery to make walking for a quarter of an hour quite pleasant.

"I will, sir, if you promise to bring her back whole and take some refreshment with us." The baron chuckled and folded his hands in his lap. "And you must see to it she enjoys herself."

"I will endeavor to do my best, my lord." Oliver bowed and then held his hand out to Mattie, his eyes glimmering with humor. Indeed, he seemed *very* pleased with himself. He still wore his frock coat from attending church, but his cravat looked the worse for wear with a few more wrinkles than it should possess.

Mattie stepped around her father's bench, reaching out

to take Oliver's hand. "You have agreed to a great many things, Mr. Bolton. I wonder if you can fulfill all your promises."

Her hand, ungloved, touched his, and as he curled his fingers around it, something inside her *uncurled* and grew, tiny tendrils of warmth creeping through her as if seeking the sun.

Oliver's grin revealed the dimple in his left cheek. He wasn't wearing gloves either, she realized belatedly.

"I am afraid I was in a bit of a hurry," he said, looking to their joined hands. "I forgot my gloves. I didn't wish to arrive late—"

"It—it is fine." She started to pull her hand away, but he gently tucked her arm through his.

"Have you had a pleasant afternoon?" Oliver asked.

Oliver led her down the terrace steps while her mind tried to unravel itself from whatever strange thing had taken hold of her. Noticing dimples and feeling strange sensations at a man's touch was hardly becoming, and nothing at all like her. Had she not taken his arm at the theater? Having spent several hours in his company only the day before, it was ridiculous to think any of the sensations overtaking her consciousness could be attributed to Oliver Bolton.

Perhaps she was taking ill. But ill or not, she had a duty to perform for her family. Her mother and sister would return Wednesday.

Oliver spoke her name and his tone suggested it wasn't for the first time. "Miss Rayment? Matilda?"

"Oh, I beg your pardon." Mattie felt the blush creep up her throat and into her cheeks. Twice in one day. "I am afraid I was thinking over the sermon."

"Ah. The weighty discussion of laying treasure up in

heaven and forgoing earthly pleasures." He spoke with interest rather than amusement.

"Mm." Unprepared to actually converse on the topic, Mattie's mind didn't form an immediate answer.

"I found it most interesting. As you know, Westerwind has taken a great deal of my time these past years. There were many occasions I thought to visit my uncle and wrote to him, but he always encouraged me to remain where I was and build up my assets." Oliver's head bowed as he spoke, walking slowly on the gravel that encircled the whole of the garden. "I shouldn't have listened. He is the only family I have left, and I have lost a great deal of time in his company. That is what I thought on, when treasures in heaven were mentioned. Surely our friendships are such treasure."

The amount of thought he'd given the topic surprised her, as did the way her heart warmed to him with each word he spoke. "Your uncle would not censure you for following his advice, Oliver."

He blinked, coming out of his solemn manner, and turned to regard her with a crooked grin. "Oliver?" he said, the dimple reappearing.

Blast that dimple. She hadn't seen it since their childhood, and even then it appeared but rarely. "Forgive me," she said, drawing herself up. "But you *did* use my Christian name a moment ago. I am afraid we slipped into old habits."

"Did we, though?" he asked with an unrepentant lilt in his voice. "I almost always called you Miss Rayment after that first year. Uncle felt it was improper, otherwise."

She had an answer for that, at least. "I wasn't always fond of being *proper*. It was most unfair that when we were out in company, I was Miss Rayment while Miss Beatrice retained her Christian name in some measure."

"I can see the injustice in that. One wonders at times why our naming conventions are the way they are, when history tells us people used to be called such things as John-the-Fishmonger's-Son and The-Red-Headed-Mary."

Mattie covered a laugh. "Oh, dear. What would I have been called in that circumstance, I wonder? Matilda-the-Poor-Dancer? Or perhaps Matilda-the-Sister-of-Beatrice?"

"I doubt either of those attributes would be what you are best known for. Likely, we would've followed the naming conventions of the Norsemen. Matilda Baronsdaughter or some such thing."

"Lovely. At least I would hear my own name more often than I do now." She lifted her face to a brisk spring breeze, closing her eyes as it rustled leaves and the skirts of her gown.

When she looked at Oliver again, he was staring at her with a blank expression, then turned away and cleared his throat before speaking.

"Have you any word when your mother and sister will return?" Oliver asked, his gaze lowering to the stones crunching beneath their feet. Though they walked slowly, they were nearly halfway around the garden.

Was this the real reason he'd come? To find out when her sister would return? Had he sounded hopeful when he spoke? Distracted? Disappointed? Mattie tried to strangle her rampant thoughts. Of course he only wanted to know about Beatrice.

"Wednesday, I should think. They are not very far from London, and Beatrice would be most upset if she missed a chance to attend Almack's. It distressed her a great deal when we didn't receive vouchers last Season. She carried on about it every week." Mattie tried not to wince. Laying forth her sister's shortcomings didn't sit well with her. But it must be done. "This Season, she's insisted on a different gown for each ball. The seamstress we employ is quite overworked."

Oliver raised his eyebrows at the comment but said nothing of it. He changed the subject entirely when he spoke.

"I wonder, Miss Rayment, what you are doing to stay busy while your mother and sister are gone? I cannot think you have left the house unless in my company."

Why were they talking of her when she was supposed to be finding a means to distract *him*? And why did it disappoint her when he didn't call her by her Christian name again?

"I am most content to keep my father company. When Mother and Beatrice return, we will all find amusement enough. This is quite the respite, I assure you, and I still have the occasional caller." Of course, the callers were usually looking for her mother or Beatrice. But she needn't reveal that sad truth to him. "Do you have any plans for your amusement?"

Oliver shrugged. "Nothing of great interest. As I am new to London, I thought I would spend tomorrow walking its streets. Have you any suggestions of sights I ought to see?"

Anything that will keep you from thinking of Beatrice. Mattie forced a cheerful smile and tone when she answered him aloud. "Piccadilly holds many interesting sights. Book shops, a museum, and Fortnum and Mason has such delicious foods if you grow hungry on your journey through the streets."

He slowed his steps and didn't quite look at her when he spoke again. "Do you think there is a chance you might come with me? Wandering about on my own doesn't sound appealing."

Mattie stopped walking entirely. She stared up at him,

her mouth open and then closed again when she couldn't immediately form a response. Had Oliver really just invited *her* on an outing with him? How absurd. And yet. She couldn't deny the thrill it sent through her, to have Oliver— or anyone, she told herself firmly—seek out her company without her mother or Beatrice as part of the party.

"I'm not certain I would be the best guide," she said, trying to demure though the idea of walking through her favorite shops pulled at her. It had *nothing* to do with being in Oliver's company, of course. Or so she tried to tell herself, even while growing warmer to the idea. "Even if you could overlook that, I cannot think my company would be all that diverting. And I would need to secure a chaperone of some sort."

"Chaperone? Surely a maid would do. We will be on the paths, in open air, most of the time." He paused, turning to face her; his tone turned almost cajoling as he spoke. "Do come with me, Miss Rayment. I find you *are* very good company. I would endeavor to make certain you enjoy yourself."

His sincerity touched her, and guilt crept into her heart. Oliver was nothing but kind. If only Beatrice could be happy with his modest circumstances, Mattie would tell her sister how inexplicably lucky she was to attract someone with Oliver's good heart. But Mattie knew her sister, knew what Beatrice would expect of her future, and that Oliver would struggle to keep Beatrice as busy and happy as she liked to be. Though both had good hearts, that wasn't enough to ensure marital felicity. Beatrice wanted parties and balls, gowns that sparkled with jewels, and a life which required little more of her than the duties of a perfect Society hostess.

They were running out of time to secure Beatrice a marriage that would provide happiness as well as financial stability. At twenty-two, Beatrice was growing out of the age when men would be dazzled by her playfulness. She needed to marry, to be cared for, before their father's condition worsened.

Before we are all in the country, caring for him and hiding from the gossips.

Going with Oliver on another outing, especially one where Mattie might point to all of Beatrice's favorite expensive shops, might help her endeavor. She would need to make arrangements for someone to attend closely to her father, to keep him from agitation. If they went earlier in the day, which was usually the best time for her father's mind and clarity, there might not be any difficulties.

"I would enjoy the outing, Mr. Bolton. Would ten o'clock be an acceptable time for you to begin our expedition?"

"More than acceptable," he answered, the dimple appearing along and a triumphant gleam in his eyes.

Oh dear. Dimples really ought to be illegal.

They returned to the terrace, where her father appeared to doze until they came near. He rubbed at his eyes and smiled, a tired smile, up at the two of them. "Back so soon? And tell me, were there adventures?"

"Perhaps the start of one," Oliver answered before Mattie could respond, settling into the chair near her father as though intending to stay for a long time.

That warmth she'd felt earlier made itself known again, wrapping around her heart in an alarmingly familiar manner. What did Oliver mean by inviting her to accompany him in yet another outing? Surely, he only meant to gain her favor in order to gain Beatrice's. Right?

Mattie swallowed and took a step back. "I will see about some lemonade," she said, her voice sounding hoarse to her ears. She spun on her heel and hurried into the house, failing to outrun the stirring of an emotion she had long denied herself. She certainly wasn't about to fall in love with Oliver. Not when he was only interested in her sister.

Not even if she felt how easy a matter it would be to let her admiration for him turn into something more.

CHAPTER 11

*O*liver sat in his rented rooms, his valet seeing to his clothing for the next day and tutting over the state of the cravats. It had gone against his nature, to have another man wait on him hand and foot, and one older than him too. But Thompson excelled in his position.

"Will that be all, Mr. Bolton?" the servant asked, arms full of cravats in need of ironing.

"It will. Thank you, Thompson."

"Sir." The valet bowed and exited the bedchamber, leaving Oliver alone before the low-burning fire in his hearth. The days grew warm enough to enjoy the outdoors, when the wind wasn't biting, but the nights were still cold. The fire was certainly appreciated that night.

He'd finally done it. He'd broken through Matilda Rayment's carefully constructed, oh-so-practical shell.

Oliver couldn't think of a time in his life when he'd ever seen Matilda flustered, apart from when her father came out into the street the day of their ride. But seeing her that evening, first stumbling over her words in the garden and then looking at him with something akin to shock when he'd done nothing more than invite her on another outing, showed he had made progress.

Then she'd grown quiet after the refreshments were served, watching him almost covertly from beneath her eyelashes. But he'd seen it. He'd seen the curious light in her eyes, the hesitancy. His determination to be nothing but affable was working. Matilda didn't know what to make of him, and he hoped her desire to see him vanish had begun to crumble.

The best part of his plan he hadn't even anticipated: he found he enjoyed Matilda's company. She had a quick wit, and her rare laughter was enchanting. He saw glimpses of the child she'd been when they'd first met, and the tiniest hints of the young woman she was when he left to claim his unexpected inheritance.

Oliver made his way to his bed, removing his dressing gown and climbing between the sheets. He tucked his hands behind his head, thinking through his plans for Piccadilly. It would be diverting to squire Matilda about town, allowing her to tell him of her favorite shops and books, her favorite things to see and do.

Yes, he could only look forward to the next day with a grin of self-satisfaction. They would enjoy each other's company, and—and of course, he would eventually be nearby when Beatrice returned.

Oliver had thought it would be an honor, a boyhood dream fulfilled, to call on Beatrice in a formal manner, to escort her around town. Beatrice's beauty was beyond compare; having a woman such as her on his arm would elevate him in the eyes of society and give him the opportunity to come to know her as an equal. She'd hardly bothered to notice him years before.

Not like Matilda. From the first moment they'd met,

she'd spoken to him with gravity and even her practical compassion.

But it didn't matter what Matilda thought. His goal was to gain Beatrice's attention, and he would not be satisfied until he did. The sooner the young woman, with her winning smile and lively blue eyes, came back from the country, the better.

He drifted off to sleep, trying to enumerate Beatrice's finer qualities, but all he could think on was the flash of surprise and the charming blush in Matilda's cheeks when he'd called her by her Christian name.

SLEEP HAD NOT COME EASILY TO MATTIE. AFTER SPENDING LONG minutes of the night trying not to think of Oliver, she decided to invest time planning how best to turn his thoughts away from Beatrice and the family as a whole. Her efforts were wasted, as every conversation she made in her thoughts trailed away into admiring his laugh, thinking of how kind he was to her father, and trying to recall every detail of the letters he'd written to his uncle.

She'd never read the letters personally, of course, but Mr. Hapsbury had delighted in telling her all of his nephew's doings. As her father's ability to remember present concerns dwindled, Mattie took on the responsibilities of the household. Mr. Hapsbury had been understanding of her situation and often used the advice he gave Oliver to guide Mattie as well.

"I don't care that you're a young lady," he'd told her when they'd been bent over account books for what seemed like years. "This responsibility could fall to any person, regardless of sex. There are many who would take advantage of you, but if you know how to handle these matters yourself, you can demand fair treatment."

Neither of them knew, of course, how long Mattie would have to take on her father's responsibilities. At first, she'd hoped the doctor could help him and her time in the steward's office would be short. But the weeks bled into months. Soon Mattie found she enjoyed managing things. Her heart grew to love the challenge of numbers, the responsibilities of caring for her family and their tenants, and meeting with the steward every week enlivened her thoughts.

"I would give it up in an instant for you, Papa," she whispered into the darkness of her bedchamber, fighting back the sting of tears.

If her brother had lived to adulthood, it would fall to *him* to see to all these matters. And he, as heir, would ensure his mother and sisters never went wanting. But a second cousin of twice Mattie's years would receive the title, estate, and everything but the girls' dowries and their mother's portion.

Which is why Beatrice must marry Mr. Redhurst. He can provide her the style of living to which she is accustomed.

Had Mattie chosen the wrong path? The guilt tugged at her heart. Beatrice might have spoken loudly of her goals to marry wealthy as recently as a fortnight ago, but perhaps she could be persuaded to accept a simpler life.

When they had gone to the shops at the beginning of the Season, Mattie and Beatrice had stood before bolts of cloth. All the newest patterns and prints were put before them by eager shopkeepers. Mattie had, as always, gravitated toward the darker fabrics. Then Beatrice had taken Mattie's arm and tugged her another direction, standing before beautiful silks.

"Stop trying to hide in the corners and shadows, Mattie," she had said, pointing at a bolt of light blue fabric. "You look beautiful in spring colors. This one, here. You must have a dress in this one. You deserve a pretty dress."

"But I don't need it," Mattie had replied, though her fingers lightly touched the bolt of fabric.

"You are always content to take what is given, Matilda. Or whatever is easy." Her sister shook her head, eyebrows arched. "Sometimes, you have to take what you *want*. As I intend to do. We all deserve happiness, even the smaller pleasures of a fine dress that isn't horribly practical. I despise practicality. I should always rather be pretty than practical."

"Can we not be both?" Mattie's hand fell away from the fabric.

Beatrice had grinned back at her. "Only if we marry well." Then she had paid for the fabric, for Mattie, and sent it on to their dressmaker. And Mattie loved that dress. Even though there were few places she could wear it.

Could Beatrice find happiness with a man likely to remain nothing more than a country gentleman? Without a house in town, a carriage and four, and the ability to shower her sister in jewels?

Mattie pulled the blankets over her head, attempting to smother her thoughts. Her mother had agreed with her, that Mr. Redhurst cared for Beatrice and would be the perfect husband. Beatrice had admitted a tenderness for Mr. Redhurst, too, before Oliver appeared on the street. Her sister wanted a fashionable life, with houses in Town and the country.

And I only want what is best for Beatrice. Mattie rolled over and willed herself to sleep.

CHAPTER 12

*D*onning a lovely bonnet with sprigs of tiny white flowers, Mattie fought the desire to tuck a feather into its brim as well. Jesting with Oliver over her continued use of feathers in her head-dressing would not serve any purpose other than to increase the familiarity between them. Today she must be civil, polite, but haughty. She must speak of all of Beatrice's favorite, and most expensive, activities. It was the most subtle way she could think to show Oliver how ill a match he and Beatrice would make.

Her eyes drifted to the window, and her heart lifted. One more day with Oliver. One more day walking alongside him, even if she had to remember her motives for doing so were for Beatrice, would be lovely. His company had become rather special to her.

Mattie took stock of herself one last time in her mirror, lifting her chin and setting her shoulders into a straight line. In the reflection of her mirror, a face appeared over her shoulder, startling her enough that she gave a little leap. Then, inexplicably, her heart thudded against her chest almost painfully.

Beatrice had returned. Somehow, she'd entered Mattie's room without so much as a knock. And just like that, all of Mattie's hopes for the day slipped from her, like a teacup from the edge of a table, and dashed to the floor in a thousand tiny shards.

"Matilda, *there* you are. I heard you were going out, and as I just came in, I wanted to see what you are about and if it cannot be put off." She practically floated to Mattie's bed, where she perched with dainty grace. "We had the jolliest time in the country, but I am rather relieved to be back in town. I missed all the sites and sounds. There is almost nothing to do out in the middle-of-nowhere."

How had the room turned cold with such speed? Mattie bit her lip and studied her sister silently. Did Beatrice appear as an engaged woman? Her manner was the same as it had always been: playfully superior to the world around her.

"I am going to Piccadilly," Mattie responded at last, her voice soft.

Beatrice lounged back onto the bed, staring up at the canopy. "I always wondered why you had this room done in green. Pink, or a nice pale blue, would be so much more the thing."

"Beatrice," Mattie said, coming nearer the bed, approaching her delicate sister the way one might approach a lion. "Did anything of note happen while you were away? Did you spend much time with Mr. Redhurst?"

Beatrice's hands clenched at her side, and she grew very still. "Mr. Redhurst," she said slowly, "is engaged."

Hope blossomed in Mattie's heart, yet she held her breath as she asked, "Are you engaged to him?"

Her sister pushed herself back to a sitting position, eyes narrowed, and made a sound of disgust. "No, I am not. The fortunate miss is some childhood friend of his. A *merchant's* daughter."

The blooming excitement withered away to dust. "He is betrothed to someone else?"

"Is that not what I said?"

"Beatrice, I—I am sorry about—"

"Do not be concerned. There are other men in the world besides Mr. Redhurst." Beatrice sniffed disdainfully. "What is it you are about? Going to Piccadilly? To do what? Bring more books to Father that he's read and forgotten?" The blonde-haired beauty stood and stretched. "Just give him one from the shelves downstairs and pretend it is new. He won't know the difference."

Had Beatrice come across the room and slapped her, Mattie couldn't have been more shocked or hurt. "Beatrice, what is wrong with you? How could you speak that way?" Her sister's disappointment surely colored her words.

For a moment, regret appeared in Beatrice's countenance, but then she shrugged it away. "All Mother did in the carriage ride home was weep about Father and about me. She seemed to think Mr. Redhurst and I would come to an understanding during the house party. Obviously he was not as enamored of me as you both believe."

"He seemed to care a great deal about you, to devote so much attention to you," Mattie said, but Beatrice waved away her protest impatiently.

"It is of no consequence. He is to wed another. It is done. Really, Matilda, you are more disappointed about it than I am."

A maid appeared at the door.

"Mr. Bolton's here, miss." Making her joyfully innocent pronouncement, the maid disappeared before Mattie could give any instruction.

"Mr. Bolton?" Beatrice's voice rose with interest. "What is he doing here? He cannot know I've returned to town already."

Mattie closed her eyes and willed her heart to stop racing. How had everything turned so wrong so *swiftly*?

When she answered her sister, Mattie managed to sound indifferent. "Mr. Bolton has come to escort me to the shops. He's never been to Piccadilly."

"Oh? Go and speak to him, Matilda." Beatrice hurried to the door, her mood obviously brighter than it had been mere moments before. "I will change and be down in a quarter of an hour. I'll accompany you." She disappeared into the hall, her lovely pink dress showing her slim figure off perfectly.

"Why change?" Mattie muttered, a strange melancholy taking hold. "You're beautiful in everything. And *ruining* everything." That wasn't precisely fair, of course. Beatrice had likely been more hurt by Mr. Redhurst's duplicity than she let on.

There wasn't time for a conference with her mother to determine what must be done next, nor to comfort the baroness in regards to their failed plan. Nor was there any opportunity for her to slip away with Oliver—Beatrice would find a way to join them or tell Oliver she had been purposefully left behind.

Whatever plans Mattie had made—and they had been the frailest of plans—were dashed to ruin.

Mattie's steps were unhurried as she entered the hall and went to the stairs.

Beatrice would flirt, simper, bat her eyes, and giggle delightfully for hours. And Oliver? He would do as so many other gentlemen had done. He would bask in her sister's glow, and Mattie would shadow them both, reduced to nothing more than a chaperone.

There would be no smiles from Oliver for Mattie, no teasing comments, no childhood remembrances. No gentle words or kind looks. Beatrice would be on his arm, not Mattie. Beatrice would receive his every word and charming gesture.

Mattie froze midway down the staircase and gripped the rail tightly, frightened she might fall without its support.

In truth, Mattie realized, she was not so much concerned with Beatrice's behavior as she was with what it would mean regarding Oliver. She didn't want to see Oliver fawn over Beatrice, didn't want to witness the sight of his dimple appearing when Beatrice laughed, and she most certainly did *not* want to watch him fall in love with her sister.

Because I love him.

The realization brought the briefest beam of happiness into her heart before it was swallowed in pain and grief.

Mattie sank down on the steps, not caring if anyone saw, and wrapped her arm through the spindles of the banister.

It couldn't be love. The thought was firm and commanding. *When has there been time for me to fall in love? Surely it takes a great deal of knowing a person—*

She'd known Oliver since they were twelve years old. He touched many of her childhood memories with his presence. And she'd always admired his kindness, his thoughtful words, the respect he showed others whether above or below him in society.

Having planned out her whole life years ago, leaving no room for love, confronting it now gave her was a blow to heart and mind.

Examining her heart carefully, she dared not move from her spot.

How did she know it was love she felt and not something petty, like jealousy?

Because all she had to do was think on walking about the garden on Oliver's arm, and she blushed. Thinking of his smile made *her* smile. Planning to remove him from her family's sphere gave her pain from the first moment she knew it must be done. And she admired him, greatly, for his work to turn an impoverished estate into something better, for his letters to his uncle, and for his compassion toward her father.

"I hadn't realized you now greeted callers from the stairs."

Mattie peered down to the ground floor, between the rails, into Oliver's gleaming eyes. His smile was wide enough to make the dimple appear, and his countenance shone with cheerfulness.

Mattie's heart faltered, and she raised a hand to her lips to keep from blurting the truth to him.

His expression changed from happy anticipation to concern. He came to the foot of the staircase and made as if to come upstairs, but he hesitated. "Matilda? Is something wrong?" His eyes were dark with worry.

The use of her Christian name undid her, and she parted her lips to speak—

"Oh, Mr. Bolton! How wonderful that you are here. I mean to join you today," Beatrice's voice sang from overhead. "I only realized that I neglected to ask Matilda if we are in an open or closed carriage. I cannot choose a bonnet until I know."

Oliver's eyes had risen the instant her sister began speaking, but they dropped again to Mattie, their depths full of confusion.

"I've borrowed an open carriage, from a friend," he said, looking at Mattie though he answered Beatrice's question.

"Lovely. I shall wear my tallest bonnet, and we will be

seen by everyone near and far." Beatrice's laugh made the air sparkle, and then her steps receded. Mattie hadn't looked up at her beautiful sister even once. She knew well enough the way Beatrice would tilt her head to one side, the pose she would affect, and how she would purse her lips waiting for Oliver to answer her question. It was always the same with Beatrice.

Mattie used the seconds granted her to compose herself, so she could offer at least a tight-lipped smile to Oliver when she stood.

"Good morning, Mr. Bolton," she said, trying to take pride in her even tone. "As you can see, my mother and Beatrice have returned." She took the steps down slowly, deliberately. His nearness would not have the slightest effect on her. She could not allow it. He mustn't even suspect what she herself had only learned a moment ago.

His eyebrows pulled downward. "Miss Rayment," he said, formal once more. "You appeared to be in some distress a moment ago. Are you recovered?"

Mattie couldn't imagine ever recovering from the pain in her breast.

"I am quite well, thank you. If you will excuse me, I need to inform my maid we will not need her services." She started to walk around him, calling forth every lesson on deportment she could remember to keep moving without stumbling.

A strong, warm hand closed gently around her arm, halting Mattie in her steps. Looking up into Oliver's concerned eyes, Mattie's heart gave a hard twist.

Why? Why must this happen now?

"You are troubled." It wasn't a question, not the way he spoke it and certainly not with the way he stared intently at her, as though trying to see into her very soul. "We needn't go today, if you need to remain home," he added, his voice softening. "Is it your father? Or something to do with your sister—"

"No," she said, cutting him off as quickly as she could. Discussing Beatrice with Oliver was the very last thing she wished to do. "No, Papa is well. Beatrice is too." She gently tugged her arm away from him. "I didn't sleep well last night. I am a little fatigued." It wasn't a complete lie, but it was the best excuse she could summon at the moment. "The spring air will restore me to rights, I'm certain." Mattie forced her lips upward in a smile.

He appeared more uncertain. "Miss Rayment—"

"Excuse me. I shall only be a moment." She turned and walked away, measuring each step while the click of her heels against the ground echoed in the hall.

CHAPTER 13

he pleasant morning Oliver expected to spend in Matilda's company took on a decidedly different shape with Beatrice present. For one thing, he'd meant for Matilda to sit with him at the front of his borrowed phaeton, instructing him on the best shops in London. Instead, she sat quietly behind him, and Beatrice beside, the younger woman offering her raptures over the fashions of the day and speaking of people he'd never met.

Elation at obtaining Beatrice's undivided attention ought to have filled him the moment she airily presumed to take the seat next to his. Instead, he found himself trying to look over his shoulder in a way that would afford him a glimpse of Matilda.

Matilda might've had perfect posture, but the downcast expression she wore tore at his heart. With her head turned to one side, he could only view her profile.

Beatrice noticed his distraction and glanced over her shoulder at her sister, her brows pulling together.

"Oh, Matilda," she said, and Oliver kept himself facing fully forward, relieved Beatrice might finally offer some consolation to whatever had upset her sister. "Are you ill? You must stop sulking. Do liven up a bit, or else we will have to take you home. I have no wish to be seen about town with such a miserable-looking sister."

He nearly pulled the horse up in that moment, so shocked was he by the unfeeling words. Never, in all his time at the Granthorne estate, had he seen the sisters regard each other with anything other than kindness.

"Are you unwell, Miss Rayment?" he asked over his shoulder, trying to gentle Beatrice's admonishments. "We can stop for refreshment, if you wish?"

"I am well. Please, do not trouble yourself. I'm only thinking." He heard the forced lightness of her voice.

Whatever it was she thought on, it must've been of a gloomy and fretful nature.

Beatrice made a humming sound, then filled the rest of their drive with her conversation and a few pointed compliments to his driving, suit of clothes, and the like.

This is ridiculous. I wanted Beatrice's notice, now I have it, and I'm fretting over Matilda. Enough. Oliver took himself in hand and determined to enjoy every minute of their exploration.

Before long, he had managed to join in Beatrice's chatter, asking her questions about how she'd spent the Season thus far and other such pleasantries. The conversation never went deeper than the very sort of thing one could discuss in a quarter-of-an-hour morning call, but it remained amiable. Though he never forgot for a moment that Matilda sat behind him in silence.

Even when he tried to include her in the conversation, which was dashed difficult given how they were seated.

Upon their arrival in front of the bookseller's, Oliver found a boy willing to look after his horses before helping

Beatrice down from her seat. Then he extended the same courtesy to Matilda, offering her a gallant bow and smile.

She looked down at him, her expression placid but unsmiling, and took his hand.

There's no reason she can't enjoy herself. Even if she is off balance with Beatrice's presence. But how could he help?

Before Matilda could withdraw it, Oliver tucked her hand into the crook of his right arm and secured it to him by covering it with his hand. "You promised to be my guide, Miss Rayment. You cannot do that if you walk behind us."

Matilda's eyes widened and flew up to meet his. That had been precisely what she'd intended, it would seem, to follow them about all day as a chaperone. It wouldn't do.

Miss Beatrice slipped her lace-gloved hand onto his other arm. "We will both guide you, Mr. Bolton," she said in her airy way.

Matilda focused her gaze on the street and stepped a little away from him, though her hand remained on his arm.

The ensuing hour spent walking in and out of shops, peering through windows, and nodding to passersby, proved to be one of the strangest in Oliver's memory. On his left arm, he had the young lady he'd admired in his youth, knowing he would never be in a position to do more than look on in wonder as she lived a life he dreamed of. And here she batted her eyes at him, paid coy compliments, and flirted most sweetly. It ought to have been rewarding.

Yet on his other arm, quiet and withdrawn, was a woman whom he'd never taken special notice of until the previous week. But that wasn't right either. He possessed memories full of Matilda Rayment's practical advice, kind smiles, and serious eyes looking across a room at him.

While he'd stared after Beatrice, thinking her a fairylike creature, he'd hardly noticed she never once glanced at him.

But Matilda had been there from the start, expressing her condolences over his loss. Appearing in his uncle's office to bring him a book or speak to him about his studies under his uncle. She'd shown an interest in him few others had.

They had just stepped into a little green area, to partake of a basket of crackers and jellies purchased, when Oliver's thoughts finally burst out upon his tongue.

"Miss Beatrice," he said in so abrupt a manner that the young lady stopped walking. "Do you remember when you had to learn the minuet, and your dancing master insisted your sister and I join you to practice?"

After her lovely blue eyes blinked at him twice, the young woman shook her head. "I am afraid not, but I suppose I must now thank you for those services. You must've been quite the accomplished dancer, because I haven't had even a moment of trouble with those steps since my come-out." Beatrice's eyes strayed from him to glance about the park's lawn. "Oh, there is a bench. How perfect." She released his arm and went toward it.

Oliver watched her, thoroughly befuddled. It had been one of his favorite memories, dancing with the sisters, even though it had also been somewhat embarrassing. He could hardly hold it against Beatrice if she did not remember it the same way.

"You trod on her gown," Matilda said, voice gentle and soft. "It wasn't one she liked, so she didn't mind."

He turned his attention to her, aware of her steady presence at his side.

"You remember?" he asked, searching her eyes.

Matilda nodded, and the smallest of smiles turned her lips upward. "Did you ever learn the minuet, Mr. Bolton? Or do you still require your partners to whisper the steps to you?" There was nothing unkind in her words. She spoke with the air of one sharing a jest or secret, then she released his arm and went ahead of him, joining her sister in arranging the impromptu picnic.

It struck him, like a bolt from heaven, that while Beatrice might've been the sister he hoped to impress, it was Matilda who had been the one worth befriending. Matilda, the thoughtful sister, who observed the world around her while her sister flitted about with no more care than a butterfly as she had since childhood.

While the time spent in Matilda's company that week had been refreshing—he had looked forward to each of their meetings. He had watched her during the play and found amusement in her reactions more than in what happened on the stage. He had felt at peace while seated next to her in church. Had wanted to soothe and help her when he realized just how poorly her father's health had become. And in all their little conversations, he had felt such an easiness between them. He could have spoken with Matilda for hours and not grown tired of her company.

Oliver knew Beatrice to be a charming person, and she had it in her to be kind. Matilda *had* been trying to keep Oliver from spending time in Beatrice's company. But perhaps not for the reasons he had suspected. Had it less to do with his unworthiness and more with the fact that—he thought with a surprising amount of relief—he and Beatrice simply wouldn't suit one another?

Beatrice called his name and waved, bringing him back into the moment. Matilda sat on the bench beside her sister, staring silently at him, waiting.

Somehow, Oliver had tangled himself into an affair of the heart.

He walked across the grass, fixing a stiff smile on his face. *Unraveling this mess I've made might prove difficult.*

CHAPTER 14

"I cannot understand what went wrong," Mattie's mother said with a note of despair, taking her turn at sitting on Mattie's bed. "Mr. Redhurst seemed enamored of her. Then we arrived at the house party, and the other young woman was there. And your sister acts as though it doesn't affect her in the slightest."

"Perhaps she wasn't as invested in the match as we hoped," Mattie said as the maid put the finishing touches to her hair in preparation for dinner. The Pomona-green evening gown Mattie wore was one of her favorites, due to the way it made her coppery eyes look more like warm amber in the candlelight. For a fleeting moment she wondered if Oliver would notice—but she wistfully put that thought aside.

The baroness was silent for a moment before speaking again, with some uncertainty. "But you believe having Mr. Bolton at our dinner table tonight will help in some way?"

Mattie had made the suggestion the moment they returned from their outing with Oliver. Watching Beatrice flirt for more than an hour had given her a great deal of time to feel wounded, and to understand something she hadn't considered before. If Beatrice did not get what she wanted, she only went after it until she achieved her object or was denied so thoroughly—usually by their father—that she dared not try for it again.

Papa wasn't able to help them with situations such as this. Not in his current state. Vexation of any kind usually ended in his confusion. Which meant all she could do was give Beatrice the opportunity she seemed to crave. And hope for the best.

The maid tucked small matching feathers into Mattie's hair in an artful manner.

"I think it will," Mattie said, not meeting her mother's eyes in the mirror. Instead she pretended to study her gloves. What she didn't say, what she couldn't say, was that if Oliver could love Beatrice, they might find happiness together. If her sister could love Oliver, surely that love would be more important than social status and income.

If he had more time with all of them together, Oliver might find the encouragement to put his suit firmly before the family. Formalizing things would mean Beatrice must take them seriously. Though the idea gave her some measure of hurt, Mattie could do nothing to stop it. At least, that's what she told herself, refusing to examine her feelings any further. What right did she have to feel anything beyond friendship for Oliver Bolton? Friendship was all he had offered her.

The maid curtsied and departed, leaving Mattie and her mother alone.

Her mother sighed and then spoke as though she had seen into Mattie's thoughts. "Perhaps we are wrong to encourage a match with Mr. Redhurst. Though Mr. Bolton is not of the position in Society Beatrice may have wanted, he is familiar with the family and with her. If she loved him, they might do well together. Love makes sacrifices far easier."

The words sent a chill into Mattie's heart, which jerked painfully in response. Somehow she kept her voice steady as she responded. "I confess, I had similar thoughts."

Mother stood and came to stand near her eldest daughter, resting her hand on Mattie's shoulder, almost as though she needed the support. Finally, Mattie looked up, meeting her mother's deep-brown eyes. The tears brimming there startled Mattie.

"Matilda," her mother said, her voice trembling. "I only want to be sure Beatrice is happy. And that *you* are happy. Your place in society doesn't matter so much as whether or not you find joy in your life. I hope you know—that you can understand—that is all your father and I have ever wanted for both of you."

Her own eyes growing full with unwanted tears, Mattie covered her mother's hand with hers and forced a lighter expression on her face. "You know I am content, Mother. I always have been." Did her mother hear the way her voice broke? Did she suspect there was more to it than the emotion of the moment?

And how could Mattie feel sorry for herself, while her mother stood before her with an aching heart? The baroness loved her husband dearly, but with each passing day he slipped a little further from her, forgetting things about their life together. Mattie couldn't begin to imagine how much pain that caused her mother.

"There is a difference between being content and being happy, my love." Her mother met Mattie's eyes in the mirror. "You have tried so hard to keep everyone happy and the estate running well, but all the while I have wondered if I have done wrong in letting you take so much upon yourself."

Mattie turned and looked up at her mother. "I like helping with the estate, Mother. And your time is best spent helping Papa."

"Perhaps." The baroness brushed Mattie's cheek with her fingers. "And I am grateful for all you have done to lift my burdens. But you know, Mattie, even if we lost our estate today, we would be well enough. Things would be simpler, of course, and we must all adjust. Even Beatrice." Her mother's eyes glittered with tears and humor. "We would manage. I think it's time I remind you that you are still young. That you must not take the whole world upon your shoulders. Consider your own happiness, dear. Please."

"I—I don't know what to say." Mattie leaned against her mother's touch, the weight upon her heart easing ever-so-slightly.

"I love you, Mattie. Think on what I have said. That is all." Bending down, the baroness pressed a kiss to Mattie's forehead, then rose and stood with the perfect posture many a young lady struggled to obtain. "Come. It is nearly time to go in to dinner, and I am certain our guest will have arrived."

Was there a lady in all of England so wise and wonderful as her mother? Mattie couldn't think so. And what did her mother mean for Mattie to do? Surely, she couldn't suspect her daughter's feelings for the gentleman joining them for dinner that evening. Mattie rose from her chair, reaching up to run a finger along a feather in her hair, thinking of Oliver. Then she followed her mother from the room.

Beatrice's laughter floated up from the first floor, where the dining room and parlor were located. Mattie and her mother exchanged a look, both realizing what it meant.

"Whatever will we do with our girl?" her mother asked, weariness in her tone. She descended the steps with her arm linked through Mattie's.

They entered the parlor, and Mattie's eyes found Oliver quite on accident. He stood at the window, eyes on the street below, his shoulder against the casement. Candlelight made his dark hair glow, and his folded arms made his deep green dinner jacket pull rather attractively across his shoulders. She realized the colors they'd worn were rather complimentary and blushed as though she'd somehow contrived to make it so.

In that moment, he turned in her direction, as though sensing her study. Their eyes met and he immediately pushed away from the wall, standing straight, and one of his hands raised to tug at his cravat. Mattie couldn't help but smile at that familiar habit. Oliver's hand froze and he tucked it behind his back and he shrugged, as though to say, *I cannot help it.*

"Lady Granthorne, Miss Rayment. Good evening." He made his bow.

"Mother," Beatrice said from her chair near the window, her voice ringing merrily through the room. "You ought to hear what Mr. Bolton and Matilda have been up to. I am sorry I missed all the entertainment." Beatrice giggled again, covering the dainty sound with a slender hand.

Mattie turned her attention to Oliver, her heart aching. "Oh, we didn't do a great deal. Nothing of true importance."

Oliver didn't say anything. Rather, his eyes were still trained on her, even when Beatrice began speaking of their engagements.

"They went to the theater, a ride in the park, he's come to dinner, and even church. I think, had I known you would be here so often, I would've stayed in town rather than run off to the country."

His eyes didn't waver, though Mattie forced herself to turn away. The notion that he watched her almost lifted her spirits, but then, he'd been worried earlier in the day about her change in mood.

He is only concerned I am unwell, because he is kind. Thankfully, she could put a smile upon her face that felt almost natural.

The door opened, and her father entered. She glimpsed his valet in the hall and nodded her thanks to the man. Likely her father had lost track of time.

"Oh, good evening." The baron bowed to their guest. Then he turned to his wife and went to her, reaching out. Mattie's mother took his hand, and Mattie saw the love shining in her mother's eyes, touched with a gentle sorrow most would not even see. The baron bowed over his wife's hand and laid a kiss upon her knuckles.

"As always, my dear, you are most lovely." The genuine affection in her father's voice and manner warmed Mattie's heart. As long as he didn't forget his love for his wife, his illness would be bearable.

Oliver came away from his window to stand near her. He leaned her way and spoke quietly. "Your parents are now as I always remember them."

The simple statement, given without any sort of contrived tone or gesture, endeared him further to her.

"I am told dinner is ready," the baron said to the room at large, and Mattie forced her eyes away from Oliver's. "Shall we go in?" He offered his arm to his wife, and a momentary panic took hold of Mattie. She saw her mother hesitate but then take her husband's arm.

Mattie must go in after her parents, and Oliver would be

forced to escort her instead of Beatrice. She felt she ought to apologize or make it clear she did not mind—

"Miss Rayment?" Oliver held his hand out to her, and he hadn't hesitated even a second to do so.

"Oh, yes. Thank you," Mattie stammered, hastily giving him her hand and trying not to make anything of the gesture. Oliver was thoughtful. He didn't want to cause anyone discomfort, though as guest he ought to have escorted her mother into the room, or if they were completely informal that evening he could have asked for Beatrice's arm.

It didn't mean anything.

CHAPTER 15

*F*inding himself alone with Beatrice prior to dinner, Oliver struggled for a time in having a conversation with her. She appeared as amiable and cheerful as ever, yet he sensed a more assessing gleam to her eye than he had seen before. Searching about for a topic of conversation, he settled on something any dinner guest might discuss. The meal ahead of them.

He paced the room, while she appeared perfectly at ease perched upon a chair near the window.

"I am grateful for the invitation to dine with your family. Your cook's meals are far preferable to the simple fare a bachelor might scrounge up for himself." A comment on food ought to be safe.

"Indeed. Cook is a master at creating all sorts of tempting dishes." Beatrice lowered her lashes in a way that would have had him enraptured a short time before. Now it only made him nervous. What was wrong with him? She continued, "Did you take many meals with my father and sister while I was away?"

"A few," he answered, trying to remember how many

times he had visited only to stay for an informal dinner or tea. "Your father and sister were most accommodating." And he'd enjoyed the company far more than he had anticipated. In fact, he'd had quite an easy time conversing with Matilda. Much easier than what he now experienced with her sister.

"You really must tell me what the two of you got up to," Beatrice said, her eyelashes fluttering as her smile grew. "Matilda rarely goes about Town when we are in London. I do not think she enjoys it as much as I do. How did you keep her entertained?"

"Our first outing was to the theater." Oliver paused a moment, watching Beatrice for any indication that she knew of the invitation he had extended to both sisters. That first evening, his disappointment had been acute. But now, thinking on that evening, all he could remember was the way Matilda's expression had given away her enjoyment of the spectacle on stage. How often she had smiled, gasped, winced when the characters made poor choices, and laughed. He'd enjoyed her laugh.

"Oh, the theater. Matilda would like that." Beatrice folded her hands in her lap, her expression changing once more. That speculative gleam returned. It seemed she didn't know she had been the one he'd originally wanted to attend with him.

Oliver had to smile to himself. Whatever her reasons, Matilda had orchestrated Beatrice's absence from that evening quite well.

"What else did the two of you get up to?" Beatrice asked, a true curiosity in her tone.

Oliver rehearsed what they had seen and done, the times he had visited, and fell into an easy conversation with Beatrice at last. It didn't escape him that talking about his time with Matilda was far easier than speaking to Beatrice of anything else. To her credit, Beatrice listened attentively. All the way up until the moment Matilda and the baroness joined them.

Matilda entered wearing a deep green gown that made her eyes dance, as though lit within by embers. He did not miss the glance she cast to her sister—a strange mix of hope and pain. As though she had resigned herself to a fate that brought her no joy.

Had she given up on separating him from Beatrice? But why? Why now, when he at last began to realize how foolish he'd been to want such an attachment in the first place?

When the baron's small mistake gave Oliver the opportunity to choose one sister over the other, he didn't hesitate to offer his arm to Matilda. Escorting her into the dining room obviously surprised her, but when he braved a glance at Beatrice to see how she took the matter, she appeared as serene as ever.

Beatrice proved to be the most talkative person at the table during dinner. Oliver noticed she spoke with animation and spirit, directing most of her conversation to him. No one could call her anything other than gracious. But he missed Matilda's conversation. Her dry and humorous observations, her delightful smile, had filled much of the last several days. The memories stirred by their time together had begun to emerge as long-forgotten treasures from a chest.

When he'd come to the neighborhood, it had been Matilda who took him about to meet the tenants, and she who had remembered to speak kind words to him on the anniversary of his parents' deaths.

"I am glad you went to church with Lord Grandthorne and my daughter," Lady Grandthorne said during a moment of quiet at the table. "I do love the vicar we found here in town. His sermons always give me something to think about. What was the theme this Sunday last, Matilda?"

"Treasures in heaven," Matilda answered, her eyes briefly flickering up to meet Oliver's, and he nodded in confirmation.

"Oh, isn't that the idea that what good we do here will mean collecting reward for it in the afterlife?" Beatrice raised both eyebrows. "So it was a sermon on charitable works?"

"Not precisely." Again, Matilda looked to Oliver, but he wasn't about to take the reins of the conversation. Not when he had missed hearing her voice. She narrowed her eyes at him a moment, and when he only smiled back at her she gave him the barest, friendly-sort-of-glare. "Though charitable works are certainly one way of doing good and storing up heavenly blessings. What the vicar remarked upon the most was the relationships we form here in mortality. He said that how we treat the people in our lives, from parents and spouses to servants, will determine our relationships in Heaven. He postulated that our treasures will be our friends and families."

"What an interesting idea." Lady Grandthorne appeared contemplative a moment. "But I suppose one that makes a great deal of sense. If you treat others around you with nothing more than toleration, how will that translate to heavenly relationships? A mansion in Heaven would be a lonely place without friends."

"Precisely." Matilda's gentle smile appeared, and her eyes lost some of the shadows within. "The Lord said to love others as we love ourselves, and surely that means treating others with kindness and respect, regardless of the positions they hold in mortality. Likewise, we should give value to our relationships during our lives. Those very relationships might be our greatest treasures in the world to come."

"A beautiful notion," Beatrice murmured, and Matilda's expression closed. She met Oliver's eyes one more time and then lowered hers to the table. "It is a very good thing we are close, Matilda. I should like to treasure our sisterhood for as long as possible."

Matilda smiled and nodded.

Oliver watched her with great interest. She had indeed given up on keeping him apart from Beatrice. Perhaps because she valued her relationship with her sister above seeing Oliver as someone unworthy. But that didn't feel right. At all. More likely, as he had begun to suspect, Matilda had been trying to protect Oliver and Beatrice from each other. They had little in common. Beatrice's love of London and fashion were not something Oliver understood, nor would he be able to support either of them.

Whereas Matilda's focus on practical matters, on the business of her father's estate and welfare, were far more similar to Oliver's way of thinking. Matilda's capitulation at this point also spoke to her ability to self-sacrifice. A thing he wasn't sure Beatrice would understand, but something he had found himself doing many times to help his tenants through difficult circumstances.

Oliver watched Matilda through the evening, noting how steadily she avoided his gaze. Until he tried speaking to her. "Miss Rayment, your feathers are resplendent this evening."

She blinked and looked up at him, her eyes going wide. One of her hands went to touch her hair. The barest smile teased at her lips. "Oh. Thank you."

"Feathers?" Lord Granthorne looked up from his plate to peer at his daughter. "It is an interesting thing, is it not, what young ladies will find to festoon themselves with? Although

I do think feathers a finer thing than those gaudy wigs everyone used to wear."

"A lady wearing feathers is quite the thing," Beatrice said. "I find them quite graceful."

Matilda's pleasant expression returned as she sent a kind look toward her sister. "I seem to wear them a great deal more than I thought I did, given how often Mr. Bolton points them out."

"Perhaps I am fonder of them than I realized," Oliver dared to say. "As I have never noticed what a lady wears in her hair until quite recently." Her cheeks turned pink, and his heart warmed at the sight. Finally, he'd said something to get a reaction directly from her. And that victory held incredible sweetness.

Oliver fell quiet again, watching the sisters interact, listening to the rise and fall in the conversation. This was what he wanted for himself. He'd worked hard to make his estate self-sustaining, and finally turning a small profit. But he'd ended each day at a table, alone. Surrounded by family, by people who cared about one another, and listening to Matilda in particular had altered much of what he thought he had wanted.

He didn't want to court Beatrice. He could no longer imagine the two of them living happily with one another, given the disparities in their personalities. When he imagined himself at his own table, and he filled the seat across from his with Matilda's image, his heart felt content in a way it hadn't before.

The ladies departed for the parlor without Matilda saying much more at the table.

"My lord," Oliver said once they were gone, his heart finally taking hold of him. "Might I have a word, before rejoining the ladies?"

Lord Grandthorne, on the verge of standing to do just that, lowered himself back into his chair. "You have something to say, young man?" he asked, fixing Oliver with a mock-stern expression. "Here, at the table? It isn't a traditional location for a gentleman to declare himself."

Oliver had to smile, noting the same dry wit in the baron as in the daughter. "I assure you, that is not my intention tonight, my lord."

"But it may be in future?" the baron asked, proving that his mind retained some of its sharpness even if he grew forgetful.

An anxious sort of excitement shot through Oliver's stomach at the thought. "Perhaps, my lord. There are things I must see to first, and other conversations I must have. I wonder, my lord, if you would excuse me for this evening?"

The baron's eyebrows raised at the unexpected request. "You are leaving? Now?"

Oliver couldn't help but grin. "With your permission. I have come to understand your daughters are particular in the company they seek. I should like to prove I am capable of joining that society."

"I doubt such things are as important as you seem to think, at least to Mattie," the baron said, surprising Oliver with the sudden brightening of his expression. "They say I forget many things, but I began to think I'd lost more than memory when my wife declared you were a suitor for my younger daughter. Especially after seeing how happy Mattie was in your company."

Oliver felt twice a fool for not realizing sooner which Rayment sister made *him* happiest, too.

"Please, my lord. Say nothing yet." Oliver could not be sure how things would work out, if Matilda even *liked* him in a manner more than what she'd shown. From the beginning of their interaction in London, he'd known she disapproved of him for Beatrice. Would she think him beneath herself as well? After all, she'd declared she had no interest in marrying.

"You have my promise." The baron reached out to clasp Oliver on the shoulder. "Do not be long about your business, Oliver. She's waited long enough."

"Thank you, my lord. I will go as quickly as I can without misstep." Oliver bowed. "Good evening." And he hurried out of the room and to the ground floor, where a footman helped him find his coat and hat.

There were things he must do, and swiftly, if he wished to present his suit to the lady of his heart's choice.

CHAPTER 16

*W*ednesday evening arrived without Oliver making an appearance in their home. Matilda lingered over her toilette, her thoughts distracted, long after the maid had finished arranging her hair. She held a feather in her hand, left on the little table from two nights before. She twirled it between her fingers, watching it twist in her grasp.

Oliver had sent a note Tuesday morning, begging her mother's forgiveness, along with a basket of delicious fruits to atone for the sin of leaving a dinner party too early.

Mattie shook her head, remembering how easily Beatrice had taken the loss of a suitor with barely a shrug of regret. If anything, Beatrice had turned her eyes on Matilda to ask what she made of the situation with Mr. Bolton.

Given that Beatrice didn't seem to think on the loss of Mr. Redhurst with any ill humor, either, perhaps she truly had no thought for marriage yet. It was enough to drive their poor mother to distraction.

Mattie finally stood from her dressing table and went to the window, looking down into the street. Horses and carriages moved along the cobbled road, filled with men and women in fine evening dress with little to vex them as they mingled in Society. Soon, Mattie must make up one of her number. Though she enjoyed dancing, there was little else that drew her to such events.

She missed their home in the country. Missed being busy looking at ledgers and balances, and she missed helping tenants and visiting the neighbors she counted as true friends.

Perhaps Mattie needed to take a page from her sister's book. It was best to continue holding her head aloft, smiling serenely, and letting no one guess at her own sentiments. Despite her desire to remain at home, she hadn't even proposed the ladies of the house forgo their evening at Almack's. Really, it would've been odd had she suggested such a thing after all the work she went to in order to procure their vouchers. She'd sent gifts and notes to each of the six patronesses, along with gentle promises of good behavior for herself and her sister, in order to make certain they were permitted to ascend to the ballroom.

Tonight she wore her favorite gown. Not because she cared what people saw, but because she needed the bravery the emerald creation lent her. In this gown she could stand in the presence of the royal family and be equal to the moment. *And yet I feel so lost.*

"A feather for you, miss?" her maid asked, spotting the thing in Mattie's hand.

Mattie shook her head and laid the feather down on her table again. She didn't want to wear one tonight. It would feel too much like dressing for Oliver's notice, when he would not even be present. A foolish thing, for certain. She took up her fan with haste, trying not to think of Oliver.

Putting him from her mind required a great deal of effort, considering how often she *liked* thinking about him.

Mattie left the room in a hurry, though not unable to outrace remembrances of Oliver's dimpled smile, and went down to join her sister and mother. Almack's waited for no one.

In the entryway, her family stood, Father complimenting her mother and admonishing her not to dance with any dashing young men. Beatrice stood aside, eyes turned away from the scene. Pain upon her face. How was it that a sight which brought Mattie comfort served to do the very opposite to Beatrice? Perhaps she missed the security their father had once provided, before his loss of memory. Not everyone could face such a hardship as Mattie had.

Her sister was still kind and told her father she loved him as she kissed him goodbye. Mattie watched with compassion for both of them, trying not to think of what the future might bring for her little family. They all must adjust, especially if her father worsened, as the physician believed it would.

After the goodbyes were said, the ladies entered their carriage and were away for an evening of dancing.

They arrived at the address on King's Street behind a lengthy queue of carriages, their bobbing lamps moving like fairies in the night. Despite her desire to be practical, Mattie still felt the magic of evenings when the splendor of the *ton* glittered all about them.

Ladies in pale gowns and glittering jewels filled the walkway, and gentlemen in black coats and tall hats guided them down the paths.

Mattie, her mother, and her sister joined the throngs. They presented their vouchers and were permitted entry into the upper rooms, where the bright light of candles reflecting off dozens of large mirrors made the room the brightest in London.

Beatrice opened her fan to hold it near her mouth, covering her words from all but Mattie. "I do hope someone asks me to dance. I cannot abide being without a partner for long. I do love dancing."

"As do I," Mattie murmured. Without the kind Mr. Redhurst giving attention to her sister, Mattie likely wouldn't be dancing at all. She'd become too much of a fixture for anyone to take notice of her anymore, whether or not she wore her favorite gown.

"Miss Beatrice," a voice said from behind, startling both sisters. They turned, a young gentleman of their acquaintance standing there. He bowed, despite the crush of people around them. "Might I claim your first set?" He stepped closer and held his hand out to her, his eyes barely flicking to Mattie.

"Mr. Whitby," Beatrice said, batting her eyelashes. "Yes, of course." Beatrice's perfectly pink lips quirked upward, and she put her hand in his.

Letting out a puff of exasperation, Mattie watched them leave for the dance floor. She opened her fan, more for something to do than any need to cool herself and paused when she realized she'd picked up the wrong accessory.

This was not her white lattice fan, but the one made with feathers. She hadn't noticed in her haste to leave her room that evening. It didn't even match her gown. Her vision grew blurry with tears that she hastily blinked back. Even when trying to avoid feathers and Oliver, she somehow carried both with her. A little laugh escaped her lips, and she covered her mouth swiftly so none would hear and think her odd.

Beatrice didn't need an odd sister ruining her chances at a match.

Mattie turned to find her mother and was startled to see they had been separated by the crowd. Moving carefully through the throngs, attempting to be graceful when in reality she was dodging between elbows and skirts, Mattie had nearly arrived at her mother's side when a hand caught her elbow, stopping her.

Preparing a sharp retort at being handled, Mattie faced the person who had dared to grasp her—

Oliver's dark eyes met hers. *Oliver! Here?*

He grinned. "Miss Rayment."

She realized her mouth hung open and snapped it shut, then cast her eyes about to see if anyone else was watching.

"You said you didn't have vouchers," she said, her voice squeaking at the very last word. Why had he come? Was he here to see Beatrice? Had he sneaked inside?

"When I said that, it was true." The good humor in his voice and the warmth of his hand still upon her arm nearly gave her leave to relax. But his nearness, the dimple in his cheek, and the way he gave her his full attention in the crowded ballroom made her heart and knees both rather unsteady.

Mattie stepped closer to him, telling herself it was only to make easier conversation. While his proximity unnerved her, she reveled in it, too. For at least a moment.

"You haven't come to visit or sent word in days," she said, voice lowered. Then she bit her lip. She sounded like her sister berating a suitor.

His eyes sparkled down at her. "Noticed, did you? And here I thought you were trying to be rid of me."

Her cheeks warmed, and she looked down at his waistcoat. Of course he had figured out her early motives. "I did a very poor job of achieving it, seeing you as often as I did." Mattie glanced toward the whirling couples in the center of the room. "Beatrice is dancing this set, but if you ask her after—" Oliver stepped closer.

"I haven't come to dance with Beatrice." He said the words gently, giving each one a weight of significance Mattie could not ignore. She raised her eyes, keeping her head lowered.

"If you have come for the refreshment, I must warn you, it is vastly disappointing."

His eyes widened, and a laugh escaped him, earning them a few glances. "Then it is a good thing I haven't any intention of seeking out the food."

The hand at her arm moved down to her wrist, then his fingers entwined with hers. "Will you dance with me, Miss Rayment?" He lowered his voice, his eyes alight with an emotion she could not put a name to. "Matilda?"

"I—yes. Yes." She stumbled over the simple acceptance, her body swaying toward him. Mattie didn't understand what was going on, or how Oliver had gained admittance to Almack's, or why he no longer sought out Beatrice. But her heart was aglow with hope that somehow it had to do with *her*.

Oliver led her onto the floor. The dance wasn't complicated; it was a reel, necessitating that they change partners several times. But he never took his eyes off her, and Mattie could not remove hers from him either. The skipping ladies, the clapping gentlemen, all became muted. The world around them was nothing more than a landscape, and Oliver and Mattie were the subjects of a masterpiece she did not quite understand.

She took a moment in the dance to ask, her curiosity

overcoming her, "When did you get vouchers to Almack's? And how?"

"I spent two days going from one patroness to another," he answered when he took her hands, as the dance called for it. "Begging them to let me in so I could prove my worth to a certain lady."

Her heartbeat almost doubled the rhythm of the dance. His worth had nothing to do with his fortune, or his ability to enter the upper rooms of society. It had everything to do with his kindness, his smile, and the care he showed everything he touched.

At the end of the dance, Oliver took her from the floor and out of the room. The scandal of being seen leaving with a gentleman hardly made an impression on her. Mattie found she cared only for what Oliver might wish to say, that he felt the need to pull her away from prying ears and eyes. In a moment they stood behind a corner of the hall, people still near and servants walking to and fro.

"Oliver," she said when they paused, delighting in speaking his Christian name once more. "Almack's doesn't mean a thing to me. I needed admittance for Beatrice. All the trouble you went through to be here wasn't the least bit necessary—but thank you."

Oliver's deep-green eyes studied her, as though committing every detail of her expression to memory. "I know you do not think me a suitable match for your sister," he said, his tone most serious. "Yet I must ask if it might be possible, someday when I have made more of my estate and myself, if I might be a suitable match for you."

Mattie's breath caught. "Me?" she asked, the word coming out as a whisper.

His brows drew together, and his expression turned more earnest. "*You*, Matilda. In the time I spent in your company,

I've realized how much I've always enjoyed being near you. You are intelligent, practical, and graceful. And you are honest, kind, and direct." Then his lips twitched upward. "And I rather adore your sense of humor."

Oliver wanted *her*. But of all the things he'd said, he hadn't mentioned the one most important to her in that moment.

"But is that all, Oliver? Is there any other reason—?"

"I suppose there is one," he admitted, and as he leaned closer her heart raced. "I'm falling in love with you."

Mattie grasped his hands tightly in her own, wanting nothing more than to throw her arms around him, to dance or sing in her delight. "Oh, Oliver."

Oliver grinned and leaned down, as if he would kiss her in that very moment.

Someone cleared her throat from very near, causing Mattie to jump and look over her shoulder. Beatrice stood only a few feet away, one hand on her hip and eyebrows raised.

"Perhaps you ought to escort my sister home, Mr. Bolton, to look in on our father." Beatrice's lips slowly turned upward. "Before she's accused of being a flirt." She waved them down the hall. "I will make your excuses for you."

Despite the heat in her cheeks, Mattie smiled her thanks at her sister. It seemed Beatrice approved of their match, for all that she had seemed intent on making Oliver a new conquest. Perhaps Mattie didn't give her sister enough credit for her observation and kindness.

"An excellent idea. Thank you, Miss Beatrice." Oliver drew Mattie with him to the steps. "I hope your father is well," he said loudly as they asked for his carriage to be brought around. "It is my pleasure to escort you home."

Mattie refrained from giggling at his dramatics, as there

were few people about in the foyer to even notice what they were up to. The moment they were inside Oliver's hired carriage, him sitting across from her and reaching for her hand, she finally laughed.

"It will still cause rumors, you know," she said, though she didn't much care in the moment. The words of her mother echoed in Mattie's mind. Perhaps Mother had been right. Mattie did need to take time to find what made her happy. And it felt good to be practically impractical for once in her life. "People will talk."

"And so they always will. But, darling, you still haven't answered me. Would you consider a courtship, Mattie? A real one."

The cherished nickname bestowed on her by her father sounded so natural coming from Oliver's lips. She found she never wanted him to call her anything else, ever again.

"I have considered it," she said softly, grateful for the little light from the carriage lamps. "And I will say *yes*, Oliver."

His hands tightened around hers, and he bent to kiss her gloved fingers.

Her practical side began to assert itself, warring with her rather giddy emotions. "But—what about my parents, Oliver? My father . . ." She swallowed, hoping her parents would not disapprove of her courtship. "You will ask my father for his blessing?"

Oliver moved to sit beside her and gently put his arm around her shoulders. "My darling, I already have. The moment your carriage left for Almack's I spoke to him."

Mattie laughed, relief and hope lifting her heart. "He likes you a great deal."

"Thank goodness for that."

Mattie leaned against his shoulder and felt his kiss upon

her brow. Warmth spread from her heart throughout her body. She tilted her head back to look at him through the shadows. He was so near, and he bent still closer. Mattie tilted her chin back and met his lips with hers, the soft caress of his kiss making all coherent thought leave her for several long moments. When they parted, her lips tingled, and she laid her head upon his shoulder.

A courtship with Oliver would certainly be an adventure.

EPILOGUE: SIX MONTHS LATER

*O*n a delicately wrought iron bench, encircling one of Oliver's favorite trees, he sat with his arm around the most enchanting woman in England. His wife. Four glorious months of marriage, spent at Westerwind. Their estate.

"I love the autumn," Mattie said, tilting her face upward to look at the golden leaves above them. "The trees here are so beautiful, and the woods are peaceful."

A cough made Mattie abruptly face forward again and adjust her posture. Her father sat a few feet away from them upon a stool, sketchbook in hand. "You must stop moving about, dear girl, or I'll never get this finished."

"Sorry, Papa." Mattie smiled sheepishly, and Oliver tightened his arm around her into an embrace. She glared at him from the corner of her eye. "This horrid husband of mine keeps distracting me."

Oliver couldn't help but laugh. "Rubbish. You were distracted by the trees."

"But they are *your* trees."

"Our trees, Mattie darling." He kissed her temple.

"Ours." Another cough meant Oliver had moved about too much, so he faced forward again, giving his father-in-law a content smile to sketch rather than the wide grin he'd bestowed on his wife.

The baron and baroness had come for a short visit that had lengthened from a week's stay to a fortnight's. Oliver didn't mind in the least. He adored his in-laws and hoped they would stay long enough for his uncle to join them in another week. Of course, one of the reasons for the extension in their holiday had everything to do with the gentleman walking arm-in-arm with Beatrice through the trees at that very moment.

Robert Dunwilde, Oliver's friend and heir to an earldom, had met Beatrice at Oliver and Mattie's wedding. He'd not been all that impressed with her, at first. A fact which drove Beatrice to distraction, according to Mattie. For the first time in her life, Beatrice had to work at earning the good opinion of a handsome bachelor. Now, as Oliver watched them approach from their walk, he had to lean a little closer to Mattie.

"I think your sister is taken with Dunwilde."

"That is no secret," Mattie murmured back to him, her eyes flitting up to take in the approaching pair. "Though she has certainly tempered her flirting. I cannot think of a time I have seen her so serious in conversation."

"It is strange. I would have told you his temperament was similar to hers, always on the lookout for fun." Oliver settled more closely against his wife. "That did mean she had to work all the harder to gain his notice."

Lady Granthorne sat on a quilt beneath a tree, reading quietly. Oliver hoped his mother-in-law found peace while visiting Westerwind. He had done all he could to alleviate her worries about what would happen when the baron was no longer capable of remembering things. He had given them their own rooms, a permanent place, in his home. He'd promised places to all their most loyal servants, too, so that those the baron knew would continue to assist him. They could bring their furnishing to his home, to surround the baron with all the familiar items they could.

Both the baron and baroness would have all the comforts he and Mattie could give them.

"There now." Lord Granthorne rose from his seat and brought his sketchbook to them, a delighted smile on his face. "Despite the lack of cooperation by my two subjects, I think we have a finished portrait."

Mattie took the sketchbook in hand, and her eyes immediately flooded with tears. Oliver chuckled. "It isn't that terrible, Mattie-girl."

"Oh, of course not." She sniffled and wiped at her eyes with one hand. "It's beautiful. Look how happy we are." Yet her tears came faster as she handed the book to Oliver. He studied it, noting the fine details of her curling hair and the dimple in his cheek he'd rather hated until Mattie admitted her great fondness for it. His finger traced the feather she'd tucked behind her ear when they'd found it on their walk earlier in the day.

He'd never see a feather without thinking of her when they met in the study, her expression so serious even while that bit of fluff waved about in her hair.

How he loved that memory now. And all those that followed in which they were together.

"It's wonderful, my lord. I will frame it for my study, if you do not mind?"

"Not at all." The baron took the sketchbook back and fixed his daughter with a knowing smile. "I suppose you haven't told him yet?"

Mattie had retrieved a handkerchief, which she used to dab at her eyes. "What?" She appeared somewhat alarmed. "What am I meant to have told Oliver?"

The baron shook his head. "I know quite well that I forget things," he said with a sad, soft smile. "But I'm not about to forget being a grandfather anytime soon."

Oliver's whole body experienced an electric shock, and he turned to take both Mattie's shoulders in his hands. "Mattie—are you—? Are we—?" He couldn't quite get the words out.

Dunwilde and Beatrice had arrived in time to hear Oliver's inept questioning, but he didn't much care. All he could do was stare into his bride's eyes, watching as a shaky smile appeared on her lovely face.

"I don't know how Papa guessed. I certainly didn't tell him. Mama must've given it away." She laughed; the sound tinged with a hiccough from her earlier tears. "Yes, Oliver. We are having a baby."

Beatrice gasped. "Oh, this means I'm going to be an auntie! I have always wanted to be an aunt. I shall spoil your child judiciously."

"Congratulations, Bolton." Dunwilde grinned as he spoke, then sent a speculative look at Beatrice. "This is a joyful moment, indeed. One hopes there are many more to come."

Oliver folded Mattie in his arms, his heart full of gladness and love. "This is wonderful. I cannot imagine anything more perfect than this moment. I love you, Mattie. Thank you for this new adventure."

She snuggled close against his chest, her happy eliciting a warmth within his heart. "I love you, Oliver. Always."

Oliver would forever be grateful he had gone from a most unsuitable suitor to a happily wedded husband.

IF YOU'VE ENJOYED THIS SHORT AND SWEET ROMANCE, BE SURE to check out Sally's other titles here. You might especially enjoy her friends-to-more book *Discovering Grace,* part of Sally's Inglewood Romance series.

You are also invited to join Sally's newsletter list, so you can stay informed about upcoming releases and learn all the best background information.

AUTHOR'S NOTE

If this story seems familiar, that could be for a few reasons. The first is that it was inspired by the beautiful film *Sabrina*, starring Audrey Hepburn. Yes, I know the other version, and I like it, too. But nothing compares to Audrey in a film.

Another reason you might recognize this tale is because an earlier version of it was published in March 2019, in the Timeless Regency Collection *An Evening at Almack's*. The rights to this story have sense reverted back to me (the author), and I decided to increase the length of a few scenes, edit out a few tiny mistakes, and add a short and sweet epilogue. If you've read the story before, I hope you'll find it improved.

This story briefly touches on Alzheimer's disease, as it would have been seen and treated during that time period. At least, how loving family members would have treated it. The sad reality of the time period is that most families who experienced this would have put the person affected into a group home or hospital, where they would've likely received very little attention, let alone helpful treatment.

Alzheimer's disease is classified as "very common," in

our day and age, and there are several different ways it manifests. I absolutely do not take this disease lightly. My intent with how I have portrayed of this serious disease in this book was to treat the subject with respect, touch upon it only lightly, and show how responsible loved ones of that particular time period would have seen the situation.

Thank you for the time spent in this story with my characters. I hope you enjoyed their love story.

I also want to thank my sisters, Molly Holt and Carri Flores, for reading through this work and helping me edit it to where it is now. These two ladies have been a great support to my writing career.

Many thanks also to Heather B. Moore of Mirror Press for inviting me to contribute the earlier version of this story to a Timeless Regency Collection.

As always, I am grateful to my husband and children for their support. Without their understanding and love, we wouldn't be in our current home, and I wouldn't be publishing yet another romance. I love the happily ever after we are building together.

Thanks also go to my best friend, Shaela Kay, who designed this gorgeous cover for me. She makes all my books look amazing, and I am grateful that we have a wonderful personal relationship as well as a thriving business partnership.

If you'd like to keep up on my work, and get all the inside scoops about past and upcoming titles, please join me on Facebook! Sally's Sweet Romance Fans is a thriving community, and I'd love to have you join us!

ABOUT THE AUTHOR

Since Jane Austen isn't releasing any new titles, Sally decided to try her hand at writing a few. Those attempts led to a happy career doing what she loves most: telling love stories.

Sally Britton, her husband, their four incredible children, their dog Izzie, and the cat Willow who tolerates them, live in Oklahoma.

Sally started writing on her mother's electric typewriter when she was fourteen years old. Reading her way through Jane Austen, Louisa May Alcott, and L.M. Montgomery, Sally fell love with the elegant, complex world of centuries past.

In 2007, Sally earned a bachelor's in English from Brigham Young University. She met and married her husband not long after, and they're quite busy living happily ever after.

All of Sally's published works are available on Amazon.com and you can connect with Sally and sign up for her newsletter on her website, AuthorSallyBritton.com.

37911543R00088